STRANGE ADVENTURES

STRANGE ADVENTURES

AUTHOR: Ken Blanton

Strange Adventures

Copyright © 2019 by Ken Blanton. All rights reserved.

No part of this publication may be reproduced, stored in a retrieval system or transmitted in any way by any means, electronic, mechanical, photocopy, recording or otherwise without the prior permission of the author except as provided by USA copyright law.

This novel is a work of fiction. Names, descriptions, entities, and incidents included in the story are products of the author's imagination. Any resemblance to actual persons, events, and entities is entirely coincidental.

The opinions expressed by the author are not necessarily those of URLink Print and Media.

1603 Capitol Ave., Suite 310 Cheyenne, Wyoming USA 82001
1-888-980-6523 | admin@urlinkpublishing.com

URLink Print and Media is committed to excellence in the publishing industry.

Book design copyright © 2019 by URLink Print and Media. All rights reserved.

Published in the United States of America

ISBN 978-1-64367-793-4 (Paperback)
ISBN 978-1-64367-794-1 (Hardback)
ISBN 978-1-64367-792-7 (Digital)

22.08.19

Acknowledgments

This is to acknowledge my sister, Rebecca Ann, for all her love and support during the development of this book

Contents

Preface 9

Chapter 1: The Large Footprint 11

Chapter 2: A Visit To Grandma's House 23

Chapter 3: Stars That Go Zoom 35

Chapter 4: The Full Moon Over The Baseball Field 41

Chapter 5: Triangle Fishing 48

Chapter 6: The Long Way home 64

Chapter 7: House For Sale 75

Chapter 8: Night Sky Over Dallas 84

Preface

There are many unexplainable happenings in this world. When we become entangled in the midst of a weird or unbelievable situation, it tends to addle the mind and shake our reality as one might believe it to be. The very thought that such things might, or could, happen to us often makes our blood run cold and shakes our known world. People with faith in God are rarely shaken. They reason weird occurrences away as if they did not happen, or they keep their wits about them and ask God for protection and understanding.

The author believes that the fallen angels are the originators and maybe the pilots of the haunted house and strange lights and craft respectively. Those things are to serve to shake one's faith in God.

It is also the author's belief that an evil craft was captured as planned in the 1940s, and the government has used some of the technology to generate most, if not all, of the innovative leaps and bounds in many technologies since that time. All things have a price or payment due. I wonder the price to be paid and by whom. I believe I know a simple answer to this question.

I am hopeful this book will be entertaining and a joy to read for all who opens the cover. John actually experienced these situations. John survived it all and somehow put each episode of strange happenings in the back of his mind to sort out later. Letting some of his strange adventures be written in a book was his way of dealing with it all and sharing them with others. He hoped that others would be enlightened that other people have actually experienced those types of strange adventures. All of these adventures are true and actually occurred. The names were changed to protect the innocent and guilty alike.

1
THE LARGE FOOTPRINT

It was a sultry night in the midwestern hill country in the month of June. The year was 1957. It was a much simpler time in the countryside. Bert was a very strong, dark tanned, and handsome country boy. He was on his way home from his girlfriend's house. He was recalling the few hours he had spent with his girlfriend, Alice, on her parent's porch swing this evening. The swing would squeak as it went back and forth, as they would flirt with each other and discuss what they expected of their senior year of high school. The senior year would start in the coming month of August and would be their last school year together. Bert was very athletic and had signed up to play baseball for the summer league. The games were played each Sunday at the township ball field. Alice would attend every game she possibly could, as she thought he was the greatest! Alice had been a cheerleader in her junior year of school and planned to continue on the cheerleading squad during her senior year. Alice was a beautiful young lady with blond hair and a tall thin body. Bert has told her that all the curves were in the right places. He told her that when something was said about her being skinny. Bert's appreciation and support of her made Alice care for him more, and they were growing ever so close together.

They had briefly discussed the possibility of marriage after their high school graduation. They were keeping it quiet until they felt that the time was right. They had agreed to keep the news from their parents and friends until they were about to graduate high school. Everyone seemed to picture them together and expected that they would be married one day. It would be no surprise to anyone who knew them if their marriage were to be announced. They always took chairs next to each other in Sunday School class and always sat together during church services.

Bert was wonderful in Alice's eyes, and she loved to watch him play baseball and other sports. She tried to be there at the racetrack every Saturday night to watch Bert race his stock car. Bert worked on his stock car most nights through the week and would enter and race on Saturdays. With the sports schedule Bert had developed, he had very little time to spend with Alice. This night he had spent more time with her in the swing than her parents approved. Alice's mom came to the door and told Alice to say goodnight and come inside for the night. Alice nodded, and Bert promptly said goodnight to her mom and to Alice, as she followed him to his car. Once at his shiny car, he rolled down the two back windows to completely open up his car for the ride home of several miles.

There was no breeze this night and his car would be hot, and the leather seats would make him sweat. He loved his 1955 Dodge Coronet that was a two-door hardtop. It was black with white sides and black and white leather interior. The car had a V-8 engine and automatic transmission. That was a very fast car and Bert loved it. Alice had complimented him on the car and how nice and clean it always seemed to be. That was all it took for him to become inspired to keep it spick-and-span.

After Bert said good-bye to Alice and she was walking back to the porch, Bert removed his outer shirt and rolled his smokes up into his T-shirt sleeve, as it had no pocket. Guys did that with their cigarettes often and it seemed cool to do.

Bert was finally ready for the trip home to where he lived with his Aunt Betty and Uncle Jim on their farm.

His car's engine was running smooth as he drove on the country road toward his home. Before long, his back seemed to be stuck to the leather covering of the seat back. He leaned forward to allow the wind to dry and cool the T-shirt and his back. He slowed a little through the area, driving slower than normal since he nearly ran into a deer a month ago in the middle of that part of the road. He took the ditch option and had to put his car into the repair shop in town. He did not have time to work on his Dodge and his race car too. He would have possibly missed a race. He loved racing almost as much as he loved Alice and baseball. He did not want to drive his uncle's spare farm pickup truck again for a week, so he was driving cautiously to hopefully avoid any deer that might wander into his path.

He unrolled his smokes from his T-shirt sleeve and put them back after getting one out to smoke. He lit the cigarette and continued to cruise down the country road toward home.

As he lit the match, his thoughts were of Alice and their discussions on the front porch in the squeaking swing. He was excited from the wild kiss goodnight she gave him just before she went in her house. She looked so pretty from the top of her beautiful blonde hair to the bottom of her bare feet. Her pleated skirt and short-sleeved blouse with the puffy sleeves showed off the creamy skin of her arms and beautifully shaped legs. He could hardly wait to spend more time alone with her.

Bert was hopeful the wind would keep him cooler and alert as he drove down the lonely country road.

A couple miles away from his home, he ground out the cigarette's glowing fire and put the butt into the ashtray, located below the AM radio on the dash. A short time later he saw a deer or maybe a bear at the right edge of the country road some distance ahead. The animal looked much larger than a deer. There was a creek that ran beside the road on the right side of the road, and the critter was probably there to get a drink, Bert surmised. As he came closer to the critter ahead, it seemed to be getting bigger than any bear he had seen around that part of the country. Bert slowed the car as he approached the critter. The animal started moving from the right shoulder to the middle of the roadway and seemed to hesitate. It stopped in front of Bert's car. Bert hit the brake pedal with both feet; the tires sliding to a stop on the tar and gravel roadway surface. His car stopped a couple of feet from the critter.

The critter was just standing there a few feet in front of Bert's car, with the car lights illuminating it brightly. The headlights made it crystal clear to Bert that this was not a deer or a bear. It was not any animal he had ever seen before in the wild or in a book.

Bert's hair stood up on the back of his neck as a chill went up his back. The critter walked on its two back legs as a man. As it turned its head to look in Bert's direction, Bert saw that it was covered in a long hairy reddish fur all over except for a portion of its face. The critter had a very ugly face and fiery red eyes. It was over nine feet tall and enormous. Bert noticed there was a stench of sulfur floating into the car, and he almost choked. The large critter stood in front of Bert's car only a couple of seconds. It looked into Bert's eyes with its piercing bright red eyes, sending a deep chill and fear through him. The massive critter then turned to Bert's left and bounded once to clear the ditch on that side of the road. It landed on the side of the vertical hillside beyond the ditch. With two or three more bounds, it was out of sight up the heavily wooded and overgrown hillside. There were so many bushes and briars grown around the trees that it would take a normal man half an hour to get up the hill with a machete to clear a path.

Bert was frozen for several seconds, trying to believe his eyes and what they had seen. He suddenly wondered if it would come back or if there were more of them close by. Bert took his nine-and-a-half size Converse basketball shoes he was wearing and stomped the accelerator to the floor throwing gravel behind him as he let fear overwhelm him. The red eyes of the critter staring into him was a feeling he could not overcome. He drove his car as fast as it would go toward his home. He no longer had concern about a deer possibly straying into his path. He nervously ran his fingers through his black hair. He then dragged his smokes nervously from his T-shirt sleeve, nearly breaking the cigarettes. He could hardly light the cigarette as it moved around his trembling lips, while a shaky hand was holding a flickering match.

Although Bert was driving about ninety miles per hour, the sulfur stench was lingering in the car. The lingering smell possibly had something to do with Bert having trouble calming down from the fear that had not subsided. As he approached his home, he locked the breaks and turned the wheel to a stop sideways in the road in front of his uncle's garage. The garage was close to the walkway path that went up to the front porch of the house. It was a narrow path, and there was a drop-off six to eight feet on the other side of the path. The path was steep and too narrow for most cars to drive up it without hitting the garage, or sliding down the shear drop-off into the ditch, to end up on its side.

Bert was still full of fear and again hit the accelerator and went right up the path, missing the garage by an inch or so, continuing up the steep incline, stopping a couple feet from the porch. He had run over a couple flower bushes, but they were of no concern to him at this time. The bushes would be a large concern when his Aunt Betty saw their horizontal state, with half of the plants pulled out of the ground. Bert put the gear selector in park, turned off the lights, and quickly rolled up all the windows. He then turned the ignition off, locked all the doors, and slumped down into the floor of the car. He tried to get under the seat and was under the seat for the most part. Bert was shivering from the fear instilled in him by his encounter with the strange-looking critter with the piercing red eyes and the sulfur smell. The nine foot plus size of the hairy monster was a bit too much for him to deal with in such a setting by himself, on a dark and lonely country road.

Bert fell asleep sometime during the early morning from exhaustion It was shortly after dawn when a pecking noise caused Bert to wake up. His Uncle Jim had made the noise by tapping his fingers on the driver's window. His Uncle Jim was a mild-mannered middle-aged man with salt-and-pepper hair. He was a large man with much understanding. He was concerned about Bert being in such a state of mind, to drive his beloved car up the walkway into the front yard, almost hitting the front porch.

Bert recognized his Uncle Jim's voice and opened his eyes. He slowly moved his head from under the seat to verify that it was indeed his uncle. He woke up with the fear still residing within him. He moved up to the seat and unlocked the driver's side door. Uncle Jim opened the door a few inches and asked Bert if he was all right, with deep concern in his voice. Bert nodded but said nothing. His uncle realized that there was something definitely wrong with Bert. He suggested that Bert go with him into the house and have coffee. Uncle Jim told Bert he could tell him what was up over a cup of fresh coffee. Bert slowly opened the car door to exit the car. He looked in all directions as he scrambled to his feet as he exited from the car.

Once Bert was out of the car, he continued looking around in all directions as his Uncle Jim came close to him, walking beside him up the steps to the porch. They walked together up the front porch steps and to the front door. Uncle Jim opened the screen door. They both entered the house. Uncle Jim wondered if someone was after Bert, or what was wrong, as Bert had never acted this way before. Bert had not said one word although he was usually talkative. Uncle Jim noticed that Bert was standing for a time beside a chair in the kitchen but not considering sitting. Uncle Jim took Bert by the arm and led him to the chair and asked him to set down.

Bert seemed to come back to reality once a cup of coffee was placed in front of him on the table in a saucer. Bert stared into his cup of coffee. Bert unrolled his cigarettes from the sleeve of his T-shirt and took one from the pack. He lit it with much effort as his hands continued to shake. He put his smokes back into his sleeve. The cigarette was moving up and down as his lips expressed his nervousness. Uncle Jim provided Bert an ashtray and sat down across from him at the breakfast table. The coffee was spilling into Bert's saucer as he tried to drink some. Uncle Jim asked Bert why he slept in his car, why he parked the car in the front yard almost on the front porch. He also asked him why he was shaking so nervously. He then waited for Bert's reply. At first, Bert continued to smoke his cigarette. He finished the first cigarette and retrieved another from the sleeve of his T-shirt. He lit the second one with less effort. Bert seemed to become a bit calm and decided to start talking to his uncle about the strange encounter.

Bert cleared his throat and collected his thoughts for a moment longer. He then started his explanation of his strange behavior. Bert started his story at the point where he left Alice's house heading for home. He shared the total ordeal about the strange encounter with the large red-eyed monster and the pains in his back from sleeping in the floor of his car. He shared the fact that he was trying to crawl under his front seat, too fearful to get out of the car. Bert described the monster to his uncle in every detail. Bert started to get nervous when he was describing the red eyes. The red eyes had instilled an unshakable fear in Bert. Bert was more at ease after talking about it all with his Uncle Jim. Bert shared the monster's ability to leap long distances and straight up a vertical hill with very little effort. Bert explained that there were bushes and thorny thickets where the critter went through without slowing down the least.

Uncle Jim listened patiently without one interruption for quite a while. Once Bert stopped his story, Uncle Jim asked him if he could pinpoint where exactly he encountered the critter. Bert was certain he knew exactly where it had occurred, since he would have left tire tracks from tearing out of the area to get away from the big critter. "The monster could have returned," was Bert's reasoning he shared with his uncle.

They decided to go check the area for signs or evidence. It took Bert and Uncle Jim quite a while to get Bert's car from the front yard. The garage was missed by an inch during the extraction. The left tire rode on the very edge of the top of the slope, sliding down a minor distance as the car progressed back down to the roadway. Once the car was back on the roadway, Uncle Jim opened the passenger side door and got in the car, shut the door, and then they were off to review the area where the strange encounter had taken place.

Bert noticed the tire tracks as he approached them. He slowed down and pulled the car over to the side of the road and stopped. They both exited the car, and Bert pointed at the creek side of the road. They both walked across the road to the side of the creek. They saw several bushes broken down and lower branches and limbs ripped or pulled from trees and bushes close to the water.

They were careful where they were stepping along the side of the creek's bank. Bert noticed part of a bare footprint in the clay mud located by the stream. The water was trickling over the rocks and flat slate that covered the bottom surface of the creek bed. On the bank, Uncle Jim saw the print of a bare foot that was as big as his size twelve boots, but there was only half of the footprint there. There were toes and part of the ball of a foot. The foot would be over twice the size of Uncle Jim's. Bert had let him find the print himself after noticing it was there. Uncle Jim was slightly stunned to see such a large partial footprint. He told Bert that he had no doubt that he would have been very concerned to run into such a large critter. Uncle Jim then asked where the critter went up the hill. Bert showed him where the critter bounded up the hill. Uncle Jim asked Bert if he was sure, as the hill was heavily overgrown and straight up. There were not any obvious signs that anything that big had passed through the thickets anywhere.

Uncle Jim watched carefully where he stepped as he climbed the vertical hill, looking for some type of footprint or other evidence. He found a small patch of reddish hair in a thorn bush. He handed the hair to Bert and continued looking for more evidence. They both called off the search after an hour or so. Bert had placed the piece of hair in the cellophane from the outside of his cigarette pack. He went back to the car and placed it in his car over the sun visor. Bert was trying to figure how to save the footprint to show people the size of it. Bert knew nothing about plaster casting or other methods of making a casting of an impression for maintaining evidence. He had no camera available and did not think about taking a picture of it. He thought the hair that Uncle Jim had found in the thorn bush would be adequate evidence. They thought their word was to be believed and maybe other people had seen such critters around the area.

Due to the tall grass and rocks on the hillside, no other evidence was found of the critter's visit. They were satisfied that nothing else could be found. They got back into the car, turned it around, and went home.

When they arrived home and Bert had parked his car in his usual parking spot by the garage at the roadside, they exited the car and went to the house. Once inside the living room, they smelled bacon frying. Aunt Betty was up and had all but finished cooking breakfast. Aunt Betty was a farm girl and only went to town to shop once each month for things not grown on their farm. She canned and most meat was smoked in their smokehouse. She was a small woman but stout. She used to plow with mules until Uncle Jim bought a tractor. Uncle Jim did most of the plowing and did all of it since buying the tractor. She was a very kind and considerate woman but put up with no foolishness.

Uncle Jim walked into the kitchen first and informed Aunt Betty of where they had been. He informed her of Bert's encounter last night and shared the evidence they found to support what Bert had told him. Aunt Betty strongly suggested that they should keep that stuff to themselves so as not to be thought foolish. She directed them to wash up and get to the breakfast table before the food would get cold. They went to wash their hands as she grabbed an oven mitt and opened the oven door to remove the biscuits. It rained that night, and it washed the footprint away that was found on the creek bank. The only evidence that remained was the reddish hair Uncle Jim had found in the thorn bush.

Several days went by before Bert decided to share his experience of the encounter with the nine-feet-tall reddish critter with red eyes. He went to his car to retrieve the reddish hair that smelled of sulfur, which he had placed over the sun visor. The cellophane from his cigarette pack and the hair was not to be found. Bert looked all over his car. It was nowhere to be found, including under his seats. He searched everywhere inside his car and did not find anything but a few pennies and one nickel that had slipped from his pocket sometime, since he last cleaned the interior. Since the hair sample was nowhere to be found, there was not any physical evidence that remained.

Other people stopped by to inquire a few days after Bert had shared his encounter with a few people. Bert would have his

Uncle Jim convey the story as he stood back, listening. Uncle Jim would tell them about the very large footprint he found and the tuft of reddish hair that smelled like sulfur. He would then remind them of the old Indian folklore about critters that resembled the one sighted by Bert. "The same type of critters has been sighted in many parts of the world through the centuries," Uncle Jim would share.

Bert's very young cousin, John, overheard this story. John was four or five years old when he heard about the monster/critter. In the past, John would be out sometimes after dark and feel a presence, but nobody would be seen. He figured the sighting by his cousin could explain his feelings of being watched sometimes after dark. The monster did not hurt Bert, so John did not fear the critter. John never saw one but thought he might not be frightened as Bert was that night.

Most people in the area did not believe the encounter was true, and that such a critter could be around the countryside without more people seeing it. There could not be anything like that in their county or township without it being known. They said that they had fished and hunted all over the place for centuries and never saw such a critter. Uncle Jim would remind them that there are many deer in the township; however, there are times that none can be spotted during a hunt. "Does that mean that the deer went somewhere else, or that deer does not exist" he would query. Uncle Jim would waste no more time with them and only suggested that they decide to believe it as true or not. The subject of the encounter faded away after a couple months.

The neighbors and relatives supposed that Bert had been drinking alcohol that night. Most people knew that Bert only drank coffee, Coca-Cola with a bag of peanuts, or an RC Cola and a moon pie. It was all right with Bert if people believed him or not. They could spot one on their next fishing trip or campout. They could spot one tonight.

Bert placed this encounter somewhere in the back of his mind and carried on with his life. Alice and Bert were married shortly after they graduated high school. They had children and enjoyed their lives together. Bert never spoke about the encounter on the lonely country road again.

2
A VISIT TO GRANDMA'S HOUSE

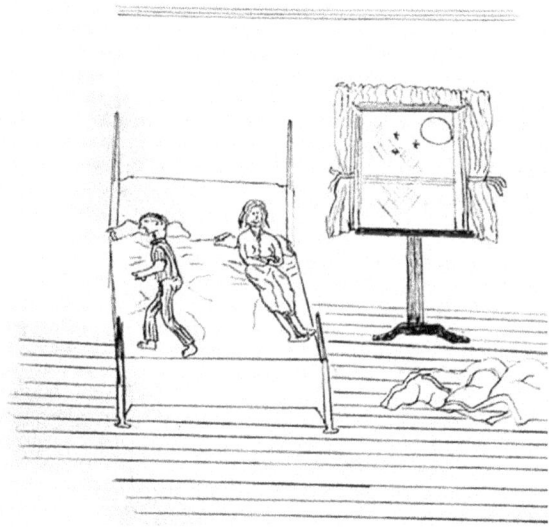

The weather forecast for the weekend was never better. It was predicted to be a beautiful weekend in the month of May 1960— spring for central Ohio and the state of Kentucky. All the flowers were already blooming, and the trees had grown their leaves back as well. John and his family lived in central Ohio. His dad's mother lived in Lexington, Kentucky, which was a five-to-six-hour trip by the family car. John was eight years old and very excited about his parent's plans to drive down to see his grandmother whom he had not visited in several years, or so it seemed. He would probably see his Uncle Arnold whom he had not seen for a long time as well. Uncle Arnold currently lived with his mother in her old red brick house in the old part of town.

The family was up early to finish packing and load the car for the trip. The car was a 1959 Pontiac nine-passenger station wagon. It had a luggage rack, which made much more room for people inside when the family would go on trips that required taking luggage along. John's dad had finished securing the luggage onto the top of the car in the luggage rack and came in to prompt all to get into the car so the trip could begin. John was already outside waiting for his mom and five sisters to arrive outside and get into the car. His youngest sister was born on the first of the year and was only a few months old. Two of his sisters were older than him, and two sisters were younger.

His dad and mom, carrying the baby sister, were finally in the car. His sisters were slow to get in the car and decide where to sit for the trip. John sat by the door, in the seat behind his mom. His two older sisters were in the seat beside him, with his younger sisters in the far-back seat. He sketched and doodled on notebook paper most of the trip. The first hour of the trip was interesting. Then the scenery seemed to be reruns of the same landscape and farms. It seemed that they would never arrive at Grandma's house. Then the sign at the side of the highway listed "22 Miles" to Lexington. Less than an hour after the sign was spotted, they pulled up in front of Grandma's house. They were all saying the trip was almost over and how glad they would be to get out of the car and stretch. All in the car were talking at the same time to each other about things to do while at Grandma's house.

Grandma lived in a big house that was built in the late 1700s and was one of the first houses built in Lexington when it was a small town. Now it is a city. When they turned onto Grandma's street, John's dad slowed the station wagon down to read the house numbers. He saw the house on the right, with a car parked in front of the house. It was Uncle Arnold's car. The right rear tire was flat. John's dad parked the car behind Uncle Arnold's. Everyone was glad to get out of the car as soon as it was parked. They all stretched while standing on the sidewalk. The sidewalk was made of bricks, and the surface was uneven. The red bricks were tight together but were kind of a tripping hazard, as some had settled down lower than the others. John's dad turned the car off and exited the car. He walked around the front of the station wagon and examined the car with the flat tire in front of his. Once Dad reached the sidewalk, the family fell in behind him, following him to the gate of the white picket fence that bordered Grandma's front yard. A couple of the sisters complained about the uneven sidewalk after tripping on lone protruding bricks. John's mom briefly scolded the sisters who tripped. Mom directed them to watch where they stepped and not to drag their feet. John was proud that it was not him receiving his mom's correction this time.

 Grandma's house was a big three-story red-brick house with big, tall windows and a white-painted porch and a white picket fence around the front yard, continuing around the house to border the backyard. The front gate was opened, and the family entered the front yard, walking on the brick walkway to the front porch. Grandma met them at the front door that was opened. Grandma saw them, as they parked at the curb, through the windows in the storm door. The screen door had been replaced to enable light to come into the front room, and the storm door would not let conditioned air escape as the old screen door had.

 Everyone took turns hugging Grandma and greeting Uncle Arnold. Then the girls and Grandma went through the house into the kitchen. John assisted as his dad and uncle unloaded the luggage rack and carried all the suitcases into the living room for each person to claim their own. The four sisters were to sleep upstairs. They carried their suitcases up to their room. John was informed that he was to sleep in a first-floor bedroom. It was the same bedroom as his dad and mom would be sleeping in with his baby sister. John put his suitcase in the room and went upstairs to see where his sisters were to sleep. It was around noon, and the sun was bright as it beamed through the hallway window on the second floor, outside of the sister's sleeping quarters. The sun seemed to hit upon a door that led to the third floor. The third floor was used as an attic and was a curiosity to John.

His next older sister Beth was almost two years older than him. She approached John in the hallway as he started toward the door to the attic. Beth and John decided to explore the attic. They got the door unstuck from the doorjamb. It squeaked as it opened to reveal a stairway to the third floor. They both climbed the stairs and saw the sun was lighting the attic through the large windows. There were a lot of steps, and they finally arrived at the top. They were looking at all the old furniture items and boxes of stuff setting around, with old lamps and odds and ends. Some of the boxes were stacked neatly, and some barely held the contents placed in them. The attic floor and contents sitting around were dusty, and a few spiderwebs were in the corners and between some of the pieces of furniture.

The attic was as big as the other floors of the house. There was a clear path from the front to the back, and they went to the back end of the attic. They saw out the back window into the backyard to see the other sisters in the backyard playing. They watched a minute and then went to the window in the front of the attic. They saw the street and their dad and uncle looking at his car. They explored in the attic for a while, looking into boxes. John backed into an old floor lamp and knocked it over. The lamp fell with a loud thud. They heard their Uncle Arnold call to them from the bottom of the attic stairway requesting them to come down. They acknowledged they heard the directive and stated that they would come down straightaway.

Beth was down at the first floor before John. She went to the backyard to join her sisters playing there. John decided he did not want to go play silly girl's games and found a chair in the dining room around the corner from the doorway to the kitchen. There was a really neat and ornate floor lamp sitting there by the chair that intrigued him. The floor lamp had intricate patterns around it and was mainly of brass. He was sitting there, closely inspecting the floor lamp and innocently began eavesdropping on the grown-up's conversation coming from the kitchen. They were sitting at the kitchen table having coffee, and Grandma was telling stories. Grandma's voice changed to a serious tone at one point as she shared her stories, providing a warning that the stories were true. She continued to say that (these are things that happen in the house during the night, but that she is used to them and is not often awakened by them, as she was after first moving into the house.)

Grandma addressed John's dad and mom, explaining that they should not let the noises of whips cracking or chains rattling worry or concern them during the night. Those sounds occur often. She stated that closed doors open and slam closed during the night as well. There will be nobody there if you check to see who has made the unnecessary noise. She also shared the times in the past that her blankets were pulled from her bed to land on the floor in the corner across the room. Grandma continued to inform them about more things to ignore during the night. She shared that sometimes a baby will start crying and sounds like it is in the bed beside you. As you try to locate where the crying is coming from, it seems to move and get fainter until it ceases. "There would be no baby in the house, and yet the crying would make me look for one at first after moving in here," Grandma expressed with much feeling.

Grandma also explained that the clocks in the house are all set several times each day as they move several hours in time and cannot be trusted to tell the right time without verification. Those are electric clocks and fairly new. She also said (those things used to scare me quite a bit, but the sounds cannot hurt you, and you get used to them after a while. Setting the clocks is a regular chore that I do as a habit now.) Grandma loved the house and started sharing the positive things about the house that made her love living there. John had heard enough and had to leave the chair. He went outside to join his sisters. John figured he would probably have nightmares if he heard any more stories such as the ones he had listened to already.

John's grandma continued her stories until the coffee pot was empty. She got up from the table to make another pot of coffee. John's mom went to help with the coffee, and Dad and Uncle Arnold got up from the kitchen table and went to his car parked in front of the house as they had decided to change the flat tire. Uncle Arnold shared with his brother that he knew he needed a new set of tires on his car. He was thinking of trading it for another car and did not buy new tires. Now he decided to keep it and did not get new tires before the one tire went flat. They both changed the tire and realized they replaced it with one not much better but full of air. John watched the tire being changed from his perch on the front porch steps. He was also recalling all the stories about the house that his grandmother had shared with his mom and dad.

John twisted his neck and body to view the windows of the house from the attic's large windows down to the small, narrow windows of the basement. John did not recall seeing a door to the basement. He did not desire to go down there anyway on second thought.

The sisters were all in the backyard, playing. Mom was holding the baby and feeding her at the kitchen table while talking with Grandma. The oldest daughter, Kate, came in from the backyard to see if she could help by watching the baby for her mom for a while. The baby was soon asleep being rocked in the rocking chair. Kate placed her in the crib and went back outside to join her sisters.

Grandma and Mom cooked supper, and all were called to the table. The blessing was given, and then the food was served. It was a fine meal.

After dessert was served and the table was cleared, all went to the front porch to enjoy the evening. The swing was large enough for three grown-ups, so Uncle Arnold sat in a chair close by, but to the side of the porch swing. The children all found a step to perch on.

The sun was almost completely set. Grandma and Mom went into the house to do the dishes and clean the kitchen. Kate followed them to help. The day had turned to twilight and then to night. The wind was still, and it seemed to John to be very quiet for a city neighborhood.

John was still sitting on the front porch. Everyone had gone inside but him. His sisters were playing with paper dolls, and the two oldest sisters were playing checkers in the living room. He saw them all through the big front window while he was on the front porch.

John decided to go into the house and sketch awhile. He noticed there was a television in the living room that they seemed to never watch. There was a radio on with banjo-accompanied music coming from a local AM radio station. Mom and Grandma were busy making the beds ready for everyone, as bedtime was drawing near. John was drawing a sketch of Grandma's big red brick house with the white picket fence as he sat on the end of the couch. He was using the arm at the end to support his sketch pad. Dad and Uncle Arnold were at the kitchen table discussing future plans and catching up on family news.

John's oldest sister, Kate, was playing checkers and not looking up from the checkerboard. She asked her brother what time it was. John looked at the clock on the wall in the living room that showed midnight had arrived. He questioned if it was that late, so he checked the clock in the dining room. That clock's hands read 2:00 a.m. John told Kate to take her pick, as one clock shows midnight and the other reads 2:00 a.m. Kate thought that her brother was teasing her, so she asked Grandma as she was passing through the living room with Mom following close behind. Grandma glanced at the clocks to realize the times were different on each clock and needed to be reset. She asked Uncle Arnold the time. He pulled out his pocket watch and informed everyone that it was 8:45 p.m. He then corrected the clock's hands in the kitchen and dining room. Grandma reset the clock in the living room. She made no issue about the clocks' time differing and reset them as if it was a normal issue. John wondered why the electric clocks did not keep the correct time but his uncle's pocket watch did.

It seemed like only a few minutes later before Mom and Grandma announced bedtime. It took a while for the children to get ready for bed. Once the children were all in bed, the grown-ups decided to turn off the lights after verifying all bathroom trips were completed.

John was to sleep on a very soft featherbed mattress on the floor at the end of the bed where his parents were to be sleeping.

His baby sister's crib was between his featherbed and his parent's' bed. His other sisters were in bed upstairs, and all was very quiet. The baby was fast asleep, and so were his parents. Everyone had a full day. His mom had placed an extra quilt onto the bed and placed another blanket over John, prior to getting in bed. He was so comfortable with his head also on a goose down pillow. John was asleep in record time. But in a few minutes, he was about half awake as he heard people talking and mumbling. A chain was being dragged right past him. He opened his eyes to see what was going on. The moonlight through the windows provided enough light to see shapes and make out certain things in the room. He couldn't see anybody walking with a chain as the noises seemed to be far off in the house. He decided he was imagining the noises. He thought that he shouldn't have eavesdropped on Grandma's stories earlier today. John got comfortable again and was off to sleep in seconds.

John was awakened by his baby sister crying a few minutes after he fell back to sleep. His baby sister usually sleeps all night, he reasoned, but then he got up to check on her. The baby was still crying, but when he looked at his baby sister, she was fast asleep. He went to the night table beside his mother's side of the bed. He retrieved the baby bottle and put it close to him just in case the baby did wake. He tried to locate where the crying baby's noise was coming from. His mom woke up and was looking for the bottle to give the baby. John told her the baby was asleep and where he had placed the bottle. Mom put the bottle back where it was originally located after she got up to establish where the crying was coming from. The crying got less and less volume and obscure in location. The origin of the baby's cries could not be determined. It faded into silence.

John scratched his head. His mom shook her head and went back to bed. She pulled the covers over her and proceeded to get comfortable once again. John got back into bed and pulled his blankets and quilt over him. He was just about as comfortable as before. The blankets and quilt flew off the bed, as if thrown from the bed by someone standing beside him on the floor. John's mom and dad were shaken as the blankets were jerked from the bed. They immediately were awakened and sat up in bed, wondering who pulled their blankets from them and flung them in the floor to land in the corner across the room. John's dad and mom just looked wide-eyed at each other. They sat there looking at each other for a minute or two and then got out of bed and retrieved the blankets and quilt. They placed them back onto the bed. Both thought that the other had removed the cover for some reason. They realized that Grandma had cautioned them about such happenings during the night.

The baby began to cry again. John's mom arose from the bed again and went to the crib with the bottle to find the baby girl asleep. John's mom and dad were back into bed sitting up with a bewildered look on their faces. John saw their concerned faces in the moonlight, and it did not comfort him at all. The crying baby sounds faded away again, and all were back in bed once again. John was tired, and once again he got comfortable he was soon back to sleep. He was almost drifting back to sleep when suddenly the door to the bedroom opened and slammed back shut. All in the room were again sitting up in their beds wide-awake. The baby was awake this time and crying. Mom took care of calming the baby and then placed her back into the crib and gave her a bottle. She got back into the bed, and all got comfortable again. They all drifted off to sleep as they were very tired by that time.

Mom tossed and turned in bed for a while. The strange occurrences had taken a toll on her ability to sleep. She got up after a time and put on her bathrobe. She went upstairs to check on the girls to see if they had slept through all the noises. There were two big beds in their room. Their mom found all the girls huddled together, consoling each other in the middle of one bed. Mom made them get back into their assigned beds and directed them to go back to sleep. Mom did not listen very long to their explanations. She told the girls that they had vivid imaginations and all was fine. The girls all said goodnight again and went to their assigned beds.

It was after 2:00 a.m. when several doors were slammed, and the baby crying was heard very loudly throughout the house. Mom and Dad were sitting up in bed when John got up to see if anyone heard all the slamming doors and the baby's crying. Shortly after John got up, the girls all appeared through the opening door. They came downstairs as they were all frightened by the noises they had heard. The baby girl was still asleep in her crib. The girls were all accompanied back upstairs by Mom and tucked in bed again. A crying baby was still being heard faintly in the girls' upstairs bedroom. Mom told them it was probably the baby in the crib since there was so much noise in the room with the girls talking while there. Mom knew it was not the baby downstairs. She was just trying to console the girls.

In a few minutes, all were back to sleep. John heard the sounds of moans and chains dragging on the floor as he woke up several more times during the night. The doors slammed and the baby cried as well all night long. All the noises ceased just before dawn arrived. Everyone was out of bed early the next morning. Grandma was apparently up very early, as she had breakfast cooking and the biscuits were ready to be removed from the oven. The table was set, and coffee was ready. Mom and Dad with all the children assembled at the breakfast table. All the children were yawning and rubbing their eyes. Uncle Arnold appeared through the back door and greeted everyone. He told them he had been up for several hours. Grandma saw the lack of sleep exhibited by all the family. She stated that she was used to the nightly noises and slept very well all night. Uncle Arnold asked if they heard the slamming doors. He then said that he fell asleep in the front porch swing last night. He said that none of the noises could be heard on the front porch. Nobody else said a word about all they had experienced most of the night. Thanks were given, and breakfast began.

They were leaving to go back home this day. The girls were upstairs packing as soon as breakfast was over. Kate came back downstairs to inform Mom that several of her things could not be found upstairs. The articles were not where she had placed them, and her sisters knew better than to bother her things. Mom and the girls went searching for the missing things. The articles were found in a closet downstairs in an old boot and on the same closet floor. Dad could not find his keys for a while. He finally found them in a flowerpot in the corner of the living room.

The car was loaded with the suitcases after all the missing items were found. The breakfast was excellent, and the visit was fine. The nighttime in the old house was sleep inhibiting at best. Grandma would bring up the topic of that weekend at her house in Lexington, every time she would visit after that time. John's mom and dad would pause and then change the subject.

Uncle Arnold told us all how happy he was to see us all. He said that he would try to get Grandma to come up to our house to visit in the near future. "She always tries to find reasons to keep from traveling," Uncle Arnold said with his hands out and shoulders shrugging.

John and the whole family were in the station wagon and ready to leave for home. Grandma and Uncle Arnold were on the uneven brick sidewalk in front of the old brick house with the white porch and white picket fence, waving good-bye. The car pulled away from the curb after backing to clear Uncle Arnold's car, parked in front of the station wagon. All were waiving as the family traveled away down the street.

Another visit was over for the family; they were on their way back home. John was by the window in the seat behind Mom, next to his older sister, Kate. He was finishing the sketch of his grandma's old brick house in old town Lexington.

The trip home was uneventful, and the family home was a welcome site for them all.

They unpacked the station wagon, ate dinner, and all were in bed early that night. They all slept very sound that night except for John's mom. The baby was awake crying all night.

Years later, the family gained knowledge of the history of Grandma's house and discovered that it was a place where slaves were traded and housed in the early days of the town of Lexington. The slaves were apparently treated very severely. When a place has had so many evil things happening over many years, the evil spirits seem to linger. There were old stories John's grandmother shared with him when he was older. One story had to do with a baby who starved in the old house. Another story was about slaves being brought through in chains and whipped if they were too slow or dragged their chains. Another story was about the way the slaves were thrown into certain rooms and the doors slammed and locked. Evil attracts evil. Somehow, the remnants still lingered. There are so many things, which are unexplainable that occur. These occurrences, it seem, are often witnessed and experienced by more and more people these days.

3
STARS THAT GO ZOOM

School had completed for the 1964 school year one week before. This evening was to be excellent weather for camping out. Three young boys had listened to the weather forecast and heard the night would be clear and moonlit. They thought it would be the perfect night to sleep out in the clearing by the forest, which was within a short walk from their parent's houses.

These three neighborhood boys had gained permission from their parents to camp out this night. Their parents could visit them to ensure that all was going fine, if they desired. Visits from their parents did not occur last year. They are older and more responsible now. They really did not care either way. John and George were cousins, and the third boy's name was Paul. Paul was a neighbor and a friend of the other two boys.

John was the oldest and one year higher in school grade level. He lived in the house between the other boys. The boys were so glad to be out of school for the summer. It seemed like a very long school year. They were hopeful that the summer break from school would be seemingly as long as the school year had seemed. The stars would be very clear tonight as the weatherman had forecasted that it would be a very good night for stargazing.

The boys gathered all their provisions into their backpacks and found their sleeping bags and flashlights. They all met at John's house since his was the house in the middle. They packed marshmallows, hotdogs, buns, candy bars, and matches. Paul and George brought canteens of water and sodas. John, being the oldest boy, packed very little in his backpack, as it would be only one night. The campsite was real close to their houses too. Each boy was sure to bring their spare batteries for their flashlights. It was almost dark when they left John's house for the camping site by the woods. Once they arrived at the site, two of the boys had to rest a minute. They had packed enough stuff for a weeklong camping trip, and it was a chore for them to carry the weight.

John enjoyed his cousin George, but when he hung out with him, Paul would be there as well. All three boys went fishing and camping together. It just happened that way. John normally was around boys his age. He did enjoy these boys' company, even though they were not as advanced as John believed he was.

The boys decided that the clearing where they dropped their backpacks was a perfect campsite. They ventured off in different directions to gather firewood. It could still get cold at night this time of year in the Midwest. They also had to roast their marshmallows and hot dogs. John brought his Boy Scout knife and cut some sticks and sharpened them for the cookout. All the hot dogs and marshmallows would slide on and off the sticks easily if the sticks were sharply pointed.

They had the perfect campsite for stargazing, as there were no trees to block their view from a large percentage of the night sky. Constellations or falling stars could be viewed unobstructed. The boys had settled in after they found rocks to line the fire pit. They had built a fire and ate as many hot dogs and marshmallows as they wanted. They had decided where each sleeping bag was to be placed around the fire, but not too close.

The boys were satisfied with their campsite and had full bellies. It was twilight now and would be dark momentarily, and they wanted to check out the sky. They all got comfortable on their sleeping bags and gazed upward as the beautiful night sky and the stars began to appear.

All of a sudden, darkness fell and the stars were brighter than they remembered the last time they camped out. The boys tried to locate the constellations and name them. They pointed out the Big Dipper and Orion's belt. When one boy would locate one, he would try to point it out to the others. They were having a great time. They all agreed that there was nothing on TV that was worth watching. They agreed that camping out was an excellent idea.

The boys decided that a contest for bragging rights was a great idea. They agreed that the one who sees the largest number of falling stars would be declared the winner. The other two had to see each falling star as well, or it would not count. They all agreed to the rules and then their eyes were surveying the night sky looking for falling stars.

John was the first to say he saw a falling star. John then said to wait a minute, the star stopped in the sky. John explained that it came from that way and looked like a falling star, but then it stopped. The other two boys conveyed their disbelief. They were all looking at the sky, around the area where John said he had verified the falling star that stopped, instead of falling. John was a little upset at the other two not believing him. John spotted another falling star from the opposite direction, but toward the other one that had mysteriously stopped. The other two boys sighted that falling star and verified it to John's credit. All three boys at the same time stated loudly that it stopped. John conveyed that it stopped at the same place where the earlier one did a few minutes earlier. The boys kept their eyes focused and fixed on the night sky as they questioned how that could happen. The boys thought it could not be an airplane that high in the sky. They had no reasonable explanation.

A few minutes after the second one stopped, John spotted another falling star, and the other boys saw it. It was zooming across the sky as the first two had done. It arrived and stopped at the same place as the others had. They were all in the same spot. The boys all looked at each other in disbelief, and John stated that it was getting kind of spooky. A few minutes after the third star came and stopped, the first star zoomed off in the same direction from which it had come only minutes earlier. Within a few minutes, the first star zoomed back into the same place it had stopped before. A few minutes later, the second star to arrive decided to zoom off in the direction it originated. A few minutes later, it came back to stop in the same place it had originally stopped.

The boys did not know what to say and could not understand what was going on in the night sky. A few minutes lapsed, and the third star took off in its original flight path and zoomed away to disappear. Then it appeared again the same way as the other two a few minutes later only to stop at the same spot as before. This was getting too strange for these young boys, but their curiosity kept them captivated. All three stars had individually appeared and stopped, individually left and came back. Then a few minutes into the discussion the boys were having, all three of the stars zoomed off in their original directions at the same time and baffled the three boys. They all three stood up and said, "I am going to go pee." They all three had their flashlights in hand shortly after all three stars zoomed away at the same time. Once all three boys returned to their sleeping bags, they all looked at each other a bit confused. John asked the others if they wanted to continue the falling star sightings contest. Paul and George both said that John won the contest. John told the boys that he did not have anything to do with what was seen tonight. He told them to not be so chicken. He pointed out that the stars, or whatever, was way up there and could not possibly see them watching.

They all discussed what they knew about UFOs and such. They knew very little. John said that it could be the government, but he did not know how they could go so fast and stop on a dime. John tried to talk them into continuing the falling star game. They said that they were not interested anymore. John called them sissies. The boys took exception to that and tried to justify their attitudes. They discussed who they should tell what they had witnessed this evening. John suggested telling nobody as they would not believe them. "They would not believe anyone unless they saw it for themselves. If we were to tell anyone, let it be our parents," John strongly suggested.

The issue was discussed a short time longer, and then the boys decided to relax on their sleeping bags. The next thing John knew, it was the next morning with the sun about to rise. The morning dew had given John a slight chill, which had awakened him with a slight shiver, as he found himself on top of his sleeping bag with his clothes damp. Paul was the second to wake a few minutes later. He started throwing marshmallows at George, trying to wake him. George was hit on his cheek, nose, and forehead before he was awakened to Paul and John's laughter. They sat on their sleeping bags, trying to fully awaken. Paul brought up the subject of the stars that zoomed around the sky last night and stopped on a dime. They all decided to tell their parents about what they saw.

When they each arrived home and told their parents what they witnessed last night, they were discredited.

"The atmosphere caused things to look different and distorted things," was the grown-up's statement. The boys, all three, decided to not tell anyone else about what they saw that night. They camped out several more times that summer but never saw the stars that zoomed and stopped on a dime ever again.

John appreciated that the night skies have a majestic beauty and much to see. He wondered if anyone else had witnessed the stars that do strange things as the ones he experienced that night. If anyone had, they probably would not share the experience with anyone for the same reasons the boys decided to keep it to themselves.

4

THE FULL MOON OVER THE BASEBALL FIELD

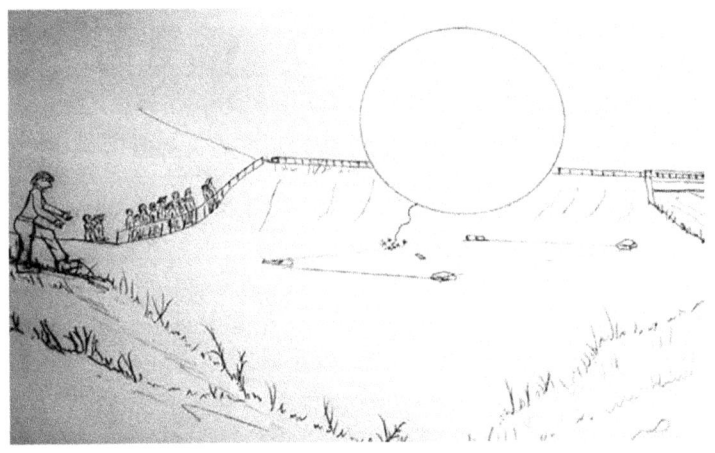

In the early summer in the year 1965, in a suburb in the Midwest, it was another average Sunday afternoon at the Roger's home. The family was having a full but average day, going to attend their church services, and visiting afterward with friends and relatives. The Roger's family arrived home at around 3:00 p.m. on this particular day and had dinner. Mr. Rogers decided to settle with the newspaper on the sofa. Sundays were the only day he could rest and read the paper and watch the television afterward, mostly without interruption.

Four of their six children had gained permission and were away at friends' houses, visiting with them and spending the night. School was out, and the children had nothing planned the next day. Two of the children stayed at home with their mom and dad to watch a couple programs that were scheduled for Sunday evening television. Dad was finished with the newspaper, and having turned the television on, he was busy adjusting the antenna that was on the top of the television cabinet. It was time for a well-liked western show to come on, and he was trying to acquire a clear picture on the screen.

Mrs. Rogers was doing the supper dishes and cleaning the table of dishes and leftover food. Mrs. Rogers had just placed several dirty dishes into hot water in the sink for washing when the wall phone rang. Mrs. Rogers answered the phone and recognized her sister's voice, speaking frantically about something. Her sister Maggie was very excited about something.

Mrs. Rogers asked her frantic sister if she had been drinking the cooking sherry, as her sister was acting very strange. Her sister finally calmed down to explain that she is presently viewing a big UFO, and it was about to land into her backyard. Her sister then conveyed that it was starting to move away in the direction of her house as if following the phone line. Maggie demanded that her sister get off the phone and look in the direction of her house several miles away. Maggie was certain the UFO was coming toward Mrs. Roger's house. Maggie was certain that her sister could see the UFO from her backyard.

During the phone conversation, Mrs. Rogers noticed her twelve-year- old son had appeared in the kitchen, eavesdropping on the contents of the discussion. He could only hear one side of the conversation, but he became very interested in the odd statements and questions his mom was voicing. His mom had repeated most of the conversation out loud, not believing what she was hearing. The daughter and dad were now drawn into the kitchen to hear clearly what was being said.

Mrs. Rogers glanced briefly at each of her two children and then focused her eyes and attention at her husband. While looking at her husband, she began placing the phone down on the breakfast bar, then stated to him to come into the backyard with her to see what her sister Maggie, was talking about. She said that if they saw nothing, she would be concerned about her sister's mental health. The mom, dad, nine-year- old sister, and the twelve-year-old son were all walking down the back door steps and into the backyard one after the other. They all continued walking until they reached the back fence of their property. There were no obstructions to viewing most of the sky from the backyard fence. Anything in the sky could be viewed from that vantage point, especially if it was to approach from the direction that her sister's house was located. Nothing was noticed anywhere in the sky as they looked in all directions.

They happened to suddenly spot a round bright white object in the sky coming from the direction where her sister's house was located. The closer it advanced, the larger it became. It resembled the full moon in the midevening sky, continuing to advance toward the subdivision, and growing larger every second. The setting sun was behind a cloud bank and was providing evening light but did not distort the advancing object.

The Rogers noticed that all the neighbors were assembled at their back fences located at their back property lines. Nobody was saying a word as they were just caught up in the happening. The neighbors seemed to be gathered into small groups. Nobody was talking to each other. They were just standing there as if hypnotized or fully engrossed in curiosity of the approaching object. The bright moonlike sphere was coming closer and closer to the subdivision but made no noise at all. It seemed to be floating closer and closer until it was hovering over the baseball diamond that was located just west of the subdivision. The strange object came directly over the baseball diamond and stopped moving and hovered over it only a few feet from the ground. The strange object continued to glow as if a bright light was being emitted from within, but it had no visible windows or openings. The object glowed as if the brightest moon ever observed in the night sky. Nobody said a word or moved a muscle. There were a few hundred people standing around at this time. All the people were several yards away from the actual location of the object. The object had sparks dropping from it as if an electrical wire was short circuiting. The wire seemed to be aimlessly waving back and forth with the sparks being emitted randomly.

The twelve-year-old son named John, of the Rogers family, gained curiosity and decided to advance closer to the strange object. He hesitated briefly to look back over his shoulder for his parents' approval to explore the object from a closer position. He realized that his mom and dad were not aware that he was there. They were possibly in the same trance that all the other people seemed to be experiencing. John said nothing to his parents or sister but looked over his shoulder at them. As he turned back to be facing the strange bright sphere, he opened the gate and proceeded down the hill toward the bright object hovering a few feet above the grass of the baseball field. John took several slow steps toward the bright object feeling curious, as he glanced briefly at the group of statue-like people standing perfectly still at the perimeter of the ball field.

At some point, John's curiosity faded. He recalled slowly walking down the hill and then deciding to travel back up the hill to where his family was standing. He would not recall anything else occurring.

Mr. And Mrs. Rogers stood on the hill as their son John came back up the hill. He realized that the bright object was again moving very slowly to the right and then to the left. John was relieved to see that his family members were no longer seemingly in a trance. He joined them at the edge of their yard, watching the bright object slowly gaining altitude at less than one foot per minute. The bright round object began to rise and gain altitude to about 150 feet from the ground. All of a sudden, it sped up to a speed faster than a bullet being shot and faded into nothing in less than one-tenth of a second. It was gone as mysteriously as it had arrived, but much faster.

All the people were not speaking as they turned and dispersed. The Rogers family members turned without a word and began walking back to their house. John opened the gate at the corner end of their property and entered the backyard and closed it, then joined the others. He asked his dad what he thought the object was. His dad gave him a confused look and shrugged his shoulders.

They arrived at the back door, opened it, and all went into the house in single file. The phone was still off the hook, still set on the snack bar. Mrs. Rogers mechanically picked up the receiver of the wall phone and hung it back on the wall. She walked to the sink and resumed washing the dishes. She drained the cold water and refilled the sink with hot soapy water. Mr. Rogers, John, and his sister went into the living room where the television was on, displaying a perfect picture on the screen. The nine o'clock western show that came on every Sunday night for several years was beginning. They all three sat down, and Dad called Mom, informing her that her favorite show was beginning. She washed the dishes quickly and placed them to dry. After finishing her work, she left the kitchen and came to watch the weekly show segment.

The phone had rung this evening around 6:00 p.m., and they had returned to their house around 9:00 p.m. The sun had set, and the summer night was upon them as they were returning to their house. They had no concept of the extent of time they had spent watching the moon-like object arriving to hover over the baseball field.

The phone rang within minutes of mom finishing the dishes and exiting the kitchen. Mom's sister Maggie, was calling again. This time, she was concerned about where they had gone and why the phone was busy or off the hook for hours. She asked what had been seen from their backyard. "Did you see the UFO?" was repeated several times. Mrs. Rogers informed her sister that it was observed, and they watched it for a few minutes, but not for three hours. They spoke on the phone a short time more, and then she hung up so the program could be watched.

Time had clearly been lost. The subject of the sister's second phone conversation had been changed and cut short. The moon-like object being discussed was not worth missing the TV show. She thought that Maggie could talk the leg off from a chair.

A few months after this sighting of the strange object, John began having very bad migraine headaches, which would incapacitate him totally for one day. And sick feelings would linger for several days. His dad started experiencing the same type of headaches. They both went to the family doctor, but he could not diagnose the cause for the severe headaches. The headaches would occur for no reason at any time of day. The headaches John experienced continued for fifteen to twenty years and stopped. One would occur every several years after that but would not be as severe as before.

The sighting of the strange bright object was never discussed by anyone in the subdivision. John asked several different people in the days to follow, but nobody seemed to know what he was inquiring about and would look at him, as if he had a mental problem or something.

Several years after the strange encounter, the Rogers family moved to the southern part of the country. John had graduated high school and had a job. He was going to college in the town he had grown up in the Midwest. He went by to visit his Aunt Maggie one day. It was a long time ago she acknowledged, as she quizzed him about what really happened that evening, after her call was received. He shared what he remembered about the encounter or sighting. He explained to his Aunt Maggie that nobody in the subdivision recalled the event, and his mom, dad, and sister do not recall anything either. His aunt told him that she recalled the experience of the UFO almost landing in her backyard. He was feeling much better about it since someone remembered; he had started to question himself.

He explained that his bad headaches started a couple months or so after the event. He also explained that his dad gets the same type of headaches, which he started having around the same time. His aunt was not there and could not know as much as he did. She could not answer any of his questions. He shared with her all that he could recall. She only knew that she had spotted it, about to land in her backyard, and called to inform her sister and family.

The aunt recalled the phone being busy for several hours after her sister asked her to hold on for a minute and went outside to explore the issue. Maggie's sister stated at that time she was outside for only a few minutes. His Aunt Maggie had asked the others about the encounter, and they had no idea what she was talking about.

John was the only one there that day who remembers viewing the bright sphere. Since that time, John has observed several unexplainable strange objects and/or lights in the sky. He never saw another strange object close to what he had seen that bright sphere that day in 1965 as far as he remembers. The sky has his attention these days.

5
TRIANGLE FISHING

John was finished with schooling for a while. He was really tired of dealing with snow and ice of the Midwest winter of 1972. He had been working a full-time job while carrying a full load of credit hours in college. John had saved most of his pay from his job for bills and stuff like dates with his several girlfriends. He was trying to save for the trip and move to Miami, Florida, when the time was right. He found himself canceling many dates with most ladies he knew after realizing how much more money he would have for his "Go to Miami to Live Fund." He decided that once he got down there, he would probably make new girlfriends and never see these ladies again.

Car repairs began taking more and more of his savings, so he decided that it was time to make the move to Miami before all his money was gone. He could buy a motorcycle and ride it while saving for another vehicle. John knew that he could stay with his family down there until he got set up in a job and house or apartment.

John placed a For Sale sign on his 1964 Pontiac Tempest months before it sold. He had decided to pack most of his things in hopes of selling the car very soon. He took his boxes of things to his sister's house for storage. He was going to travel light and come back for things, once he was established enough to come for a visit.

John's parents and youngest two sisters had moved to Miami less than two years before. John had graduated high school a while before the family moved down south. He sold his car one day and had a friend take him to the airport to buy a ticket to Miami, Florida. He went to work the next day and quit his job. They offered him more per hour. He declined their offers to entice him to continue working at their company, although he liked working there.

John's sister shared her admiration of her brother for his adventurous spirit. She said his stuff would be fine in the garage at her house. If she would need the space, she would send it to him or let him know he needed to come visit and get his stored things. He seemed to be all set for his new adventure. He sold all things that would not fit into his suitcases or boxes to be stored at his sister's and gave several things away, which he did not want to keep. He removed all things from the apartment.

John's sister was one year younger than him. She was married and wanted to always live around the area where she had grown up. She again conveyed her appreciation of her older brother's desire for adventure during the trip to the airport. She dropped him and the luggage off at the front of the airport and found a parking space. They met for coffee after he had his boarding pass. Time passed very quickly, it seemed, and his sister kissed his cheek and hugged him. He was directed to keep in touch and to convey her love and best wishes to the family members in Miami.

John's flight seemed to take forever to get to Miami after landing; first in Atlanta to change planes to the flight taking him to his destination, and begin his new adventure. His oldest sister met him at the gate when he disembarked the plane. She helped him with some of the luggage and welcomed him to Miami and expressed her pleasure to see him after almost two years. She had married after graduating from high school and had lived in Miami for several years. She and her husband had come to visit the family in the Midwest. Their mom and dad moved down to live not far from her and her husband a year or so afterward. They talked all the way to South Miami. John shared his plans and short-term goals with his big sister during the ride to their parents' house. She said that she could help with locating a place to rent or buy and maybe knows someone who may have a motorcycle for sale. John was getting excited and less worried about things working out as he had planned.

His oldest sister made sure he had her number in his wallet in case he might get lost in the area. She said that she would tell a few boys she knows around his age who lives in the neighborhood to stop by and meet him. One of those boys was a guy named Red. He was a genius and grew up in Miami. He could show John around, introduce him to other friends; and he loved to fish. John loved to fish also. He would buy a boat a couple of months after he became employed. Red was a couple years younger than John. He and John would ride motorcycles all over Florida. They would double date often and became good friends.

Red would sometimes overstress himself, trying to solve problems that had no real answer. This issue would cause him to become ill for a time. He would eventually decide to deal with reality and the real world and get well and back to normal. Red and John would then resume running around and meeting girls. John had been in Miami several months and had acquired a job, motorcycle, and friends. He was so happy to be close to his family that his locating an apartment was on the back burner, but he was saving toward that goal.

Red had a 1970 Mach 1 Mustang and a 1966 Chevy Chevelle with a 396CID engine and a four-speed transmission. Both cars were eye-catching vehicles and were more presentable than John's pickup truck he had bought to pull his boat to and from the water. Red would go to John's, and they would cruise around in one of Red's hot cars, listening to the latest tapes of the hottest rock group's newest hits.

One evening, Red went to visit at John's parents' house. Red waited for John to get ready. John had taken a shower and planned to watch television that evening. John was dressed and walking toward the living room. Red noticed him and sprung to his feet from the sofa stating to John that he needed to put his shoes on, and then they would go find something to do.

John nodded and put on his sandals, gesturing to Red that he was ready. Red and John approached the Chevelle and opened the doors.

After they were inside the car and the doors were closed, Red asked John if he could hear the thumping on the roof of the car. John thought that Red was not serious and said that he was not sure. He heard nothing thumping on the top of the car. Red stated that *they* are messing with him. John asked who *they* would be. Red said that John would see in a short time who they are.

They rode around listening to Jethro Tull's Thick as a Brick album. They were headed south on Route 1 headed toward Homestead. It was only fifteen-plus miles from the area they lived. Red navigated his Chevy through Homestead turning onto Krome Avenue, headed north toward Miami. Red had completed the turn and pointed up at the sky and told John to look at the UFO. He had spotted it in the night sky at eleven o'clock. Red said he saw the light in the sky, thinking the light to be an airplane. When the lights started to zigzag around in the sky at high rates of speed, John knew that airplanes couldn't maneuver as the light in the sky did. John also had no idea what the light was, or where it came from.

Then John realized the light he saw at first was not alone. There were three more lights that appeared around the first light. Then another object was noticed. It was shaped as a cigar and as bright as the other four round-shaped lights. The objects were drifting toward the north. The boys were off in a flash of speed to chase after the lights to see where they were to go or possibly land. They sped north, changing routes all the way to the Miami International Airport area. All of a sudden, the lights disappeared from their sight. Red informed John that they were cloaked and would reappear in a short time. John thought that Red had lost his sanity.

Red exited the Palmetto Expressway onto the service road and parked on the shoulder of the service road. They were parked there a short time when Red turned the stereo down and announced that they had reappeared. All the bright lights had become visible again. There were no clouds in the sky, so John could not figure how they could become invisible. Red pointed at them as the lights progressed over the terminal building. Sure enough, the cigar-shaped UFO had reappeared as well. John was shocked that Red knew what would happen. John asked Red how he knew the objects would disappear and reappear again. Red would not say how he knew. He did not say a word. This night was getting very eerie and strange to John. John asked Red several times how he knew about the lights and how they cloak and reappear, but Red did not attempt to answer. All of a sudden, they disappeared again. Red started the car and just pulled away as if they were in a drive-in movie, and the movie was over.

Red turned to get back onto the Palmetto Expressway to go toward home. He drove back to John's parents' house and parked the car. He turned off the car. John asked him again how he knew what was to happen with the lights in the sky at the airport. Red just smiled a strange smile. A chill ran up John's back. He opened the car door and got out and shut the door. John walked to his parents' front door in puzzlement. Red did not get out but started his car and drove off. John scratched his head in disbelief as he opened the front door and walked inside and shut the door behind him.

The Fourth of July was a week away, and John wanted to spend the three-day weekend fishing in his boat with his girlfriend and other friends. He had purchased an eighteen-foot long tri-hull boat that needed a motor. It was sound and sturdy. John was planning to spend the weekend on Elliott Key Island, camping with his girlfriend and fish in the boat a large portion of the daylight hours. A boat is required to access the key as it is an island and a distance from the shore. Cookouts were planned for the fish they would hopefully catch. John informed Red of his plans and placed his boat into the marina several weeks before to get a new engine and other repairs performed on his boat in preparation of the holiday outing.

Red and John's ladies were to be picked up early on Saturday morning and ride in John's boat to Elliott Key to set up a camp and ride around it all day. The boat was to be completed and pronounced seaworthy by noon on the Friday of the holiday weekend. John took off early that Friday to pick up his boat. He wanted to be ready for Saturday morning. Red had called John to ask if his boat was ready. John decided to take Red with him to acquire the boat from the marina. John had bought his pickup just for pulling his boat and hauling his motorcycle to the shop, if necessary. John rode his motorcycle home for lunch. He had taken the afternoon off to get his boat but decided to eat a sandwich while waiting for Red to arrive. Red called and asked to pick him up at his house so John was off in his pickup on the way to Red's house with his sandwich in hand. Red got into the truck and shut the door. They were off to redeem the boat from the marina and get ready for the weekend ahead.

The mechanic at the marina started the motor and demonstrated how easy it started and how smooth it ran. The steering cables were all new and functioned perfectly. The main battery and the spare parts were replaced with new marine batteries, and a new anchor rope was installed. Two new tires on his trailer were mounted, and all seemed excellent. The boys were on their way with the boat by 2:00 p.m. Red suggested that they take the boat on a shakedown cruise just in case. John agreed it was in order and also agreed to stop at a drive-through to let Red get something to eat. They went to John's parents' house where the tackle, bait, and extra stuff were presently kept. They placed water and all provisions into the boat, except the coolers that would be filled with ice the following morning. They were off to the Black Creek boat ramp. Red asked John if he wanted a hamburger and fries, as he had bought plenty. John realized he had plenty since he bought around eight orders of each and one large soda at the drive-through earlier. John thought that much food was a waste as all might not to be eaten, except one or two hamburgers and fries.

They arrived at the boat ramp by 4:00 p.m. They had decided to get bait and try their luck, trying to catch some fish during the shakedown cruise. They would then have fish in reserve. The sun would be going down around 8:00 to 8:30 p.m., and they could be back with fish before sunset and have the boat checked out for the weekend.

John got the boat into the water, and it started up very quick. Red parked the truck and trailer. The truck was locked, and Red was at the boat with his hamburgers and fries in the bag. Once Red was in the boat and had loosed and thrown the lines onto the boat, it was time to shake down the boat.

John ran the boat's motor full throttle several minutes and eased back on the throttle when they went over the color change to royal blue colored seas. The boat slowed to a stop, and then they baited two lines and set the poles in holders. John set the throttle low on a trolling speed to try to catch some fish as they went back and forth over the color change. That is where the ocean gets very deep as the coral reef stops there. They decided to eat a hamburger and fries as they trolled for fish They were not getting any fish strikes for several minutes, and it had been a while since they ate the other burgers. It was now 6:00 p.m. They were in the same area the guys at the boat ramp had caught several dolphin and kingfish earlier today. They were less than three miles from the shore. They both decided to pull in their lines and head for the boat ramp.

They had a lot of time before dark, but they were tired of hamburgers and wanted to go have dinner. The throttle was set to idle while they put the poles away. John sat back into the captain's seat and pushed the throttle up to head for the Black Creek boat ramp. The motor stalled. Red looked at the fuel gauge and found better that half a tank remained. After trying to start the motor a few times, John asked Red to switch to the other tank. The tank was completely full, but the motor would not start. They took the hose loose to ensure the gas was flowing through the hose. All the cranking was quickly running the new battery down. John said that it is a new battery and should not be running down so quickly. Red took the tools out and started diagnosing the motor. The spark plugs were first taken out and inspected. John had a spare set, and they were inspected and installed in the motor.

The boat was drifting out to sea pretty fast, and the shore could be seen as a very thin strip on the horizon. The sun was falling from the sky quickly and would set in less than half an hour. John and Red were focusing totally on the motor for longer than they realized, and it was time for a flashlight to be needed. The flashlights all had new batteries in them. They would be needed on Elliott Key during the weekend of camping. The sun was a burnt-orange color as it was setting over the water. John resigned to the fact that the motor was not going to start. The flashlight was turned on but did not work. It was time to turn on the safety running lights of the boat. Both new marine batteries were without electric charge. There were several flashlights on the boat, and none of them would work. The boys looked in all directions for the land but could not find any.

The sun was completely down, and twilight was happening. The stars were bright, and the moon was lighting the top of the water, making bright reflections on the ripples the boat was making. Both guys smoked cigarettes. They both lit one and sat back to devise a plan. Red took the voltmeter and held it on the battery while John lit his lighter to read the display of the meter. The reading was zero. The boys looked at each other and began laughing. They simultaneously started singing the theme song to *Gilligan's Island*. They remembered most of the words. John stated, "Thanks to God for the full moon."

The ocean was very calm and flat as the top surface of a dining room table. They decided that they might as well eat another hamburger. They took one out and cut it in two halves. They had no idea how long the remaining food would have to last them. They decided that nothing could be accomplished with the motor in the moonlight. They decided to fish to spend the time. Red had his line in the water a few minutes before getting a very strong bite on the line. He reeled the line in to the side of the boat, thinking he had not hooked the fish. John went to the side of the boat to get the fish into the boat. Red had caught a shark the length of the boat, and John was pulling its head up out of the water. He realized what it was after the moonlight shone on it and quickly pulled his fillet knife from its sheath and cut the line. Red made a comment about him not sharing his hamburger with a shark. They both found a lot of humor in the comment.

John baited his hook and dropped the line over the side of the boat into the water. A few minutes after the bait hit the water, John got a large strike on his bait. It seemed to be a big fish at first, and then it seemed to have gotten off the hook. He reeled it in to check the bait. Once the line was up to the boat, he felt something on the line. He looked over the side and saw the largest head of a hammerhead shark he had ever seen. It had to be as long as or longer than the boat. Red stated that it was the biggest one he had ever seen. John drew his fillet knife and cut the line in one swift move. Red asked how much more tackle there was on the boat since they were cutting a line every few minutes. John informed him that he was stocked with most everything.

John stated that the shark he caught would have made a nice pair of sharkskin pants with matching boots. Red said it could have been enough for a tent too. They decided to quit fishing until the morning came. They were hopeful to flag down a passing boat the next day, when they could be seen. The moonlight had saved them twice from trying to pull sharks onto the boat. The sharks seemed very willing to come aboard. Red could not sleep and decided to fish a little more. He got the fishing pole out and baited it. He dropped it over the side and almost instantly received a hard pull on the line. Red kept reeling and finally had his catch close to the top of the water.

John said to pull up on the pole and let him see what was on the line. A giant shark larger than the others they had caught was on the end of Red's line. John pulled his fillet knife a third time and cut the line in another swift move. John told Red that the shark winked at him. They both cracked up and decided that was enough fishing for sharks. Maybe they could catch some sushi in the morning. John's boat had no two-way radio, but that would do no good without any current to provide power. A CB radio was installed but had no power. A joke was made about using the CB radio to get a trucker to come tow them to shore.

The guys fell asleep sometime during the night. The sea remained uncommonly calm and flat. They both woke up at the same time with the sun coming up. They looked at each other with puzzled expressions. It was Saturday in the early morning, and the sun was rising. They should be picking up their girlfriends about this time. There was water as far as they could see with nothing else on the horizon in all directions. They had a compass aboard but had no idea what longitude or latitude they had achieved.

Red stretched a bit and then decided that he might as well fish awhile. He baited his hook and lowered it into the water. John passed the water jug to Red as he went to check the charge level on the batteries if any. They were zero charge. Red mumbled something about batteries recharging themselves a bit as he set the meter down and got his fishing pole ready to drop the line into the water. They both set their poles into the holders as they were tired of no bites. The sun was very hot all day; they were glad to see the sun go down.

They could not understand why no boats or tankers were spotted today. They did not spot an airplane overhead either. It could not help them, but it was odd not to see one trailing across the sky. The sea was as smooth as before and continued that way all day long. They had been using a rag and a splash of freshwater to wash themselves off a little but were fairly uncomfortable by now. They had to conserve their water as they had no idea how long they were to endure. At sundown, they checked the flashlights and battery current. All the batteries were dead. The flashlights were as if they had no batteries installed. Red tried to start the boat motor several times during the day using the pull rope until he got tired and decided it was of no use.

The boys pulled their lines in and found that their bait had not been bothered at all. No bites all day. It became dark. They had split one hamburger and order of fries around noon. There was only one more hamburger and order of fries remaining. John handed his knife to Red, and he cut the last hamburger in two. They shared the fries and ate half the burger each. Red looked at the knife and said that sushi did not sound that bad presently. The fish were not biting for some reason, and that seemed to be the only chance they might have. They were hungry and sunburned. They both fell into a light sleep from exhaustion.

All of a sudden, Red jumped to his feet and yelled that he saw a boat's light surveying in front of them as they were probably running pretty fast. Red said he hoped the approaching craft will spot them, or they could run them over. The boat was running at a high rate of speed and seemed to be heading straight for them and their eighteen-foot trihull. Red instructed John to take off his white T-shirt and give it to him. John took it off and quickly provided it to Red, as Red's T-shirt was red and would not be easily spotted. Red quickly got onto the bow of the boat and started waving his arms wildly with the white T-shirt spread as wide as it would stretch in hopes of catching the attention of the approaching boat.

John looked around for another white rag or something to wave. He stopped and froze as he stared at the bright white light that was headed straight at them, on a collision course. The boys were in a desperate fix. Red was waving the white shirt like it was the last thing he was to accomplish. The bright light blinded the boys as it came closing in on them. It was within yards of them and their small boat before the approaching boat noticed them and veered away at the last second. The approaching boat almost capsized the boy's boat with the narrow miss. The boat that narrowly missed them was a fifty-foot cabin cruiser with a flybridge.

They were from the Bahamas and spoke no English to note. John was so glad that Red spoke Spanish. John hung on tightly to the boat during the near miss but was very worried that Red would be thrown into the dark ocean. They both stayed on the boat, but it was not easy. The big boat came back around to see what was going on with the boys being on a boat out there with no lights. Red informed them that they were stranded at sea. Nothing worked on the boat. They told Red that they were on their way to North Miami Beach for a fishing tournament but would tow them to the Fowey Rocks Lighthouse. Red thanked them for their help. The deckhand threw a towline to Red, and he tied it off to the bow and lifted the engine from the water. The boys were so glad to get a tow to civilization. The guys discussed how close the big boat came from smashing them and the boat. It took over an hour to arrive at the lighthouse. It was considered that the tide was bringing them in close to shore. If the wind had gained speed, nobody could guess where the boys would have been.

The lighthouse keeper informed the boys that it was 2:30 a.m. in response to their query.

They moored the boat and climbed to the catwalk, following the keeper into the living quarters of the lighthouse. The keeper introduced himself to the boys, and they reciprocated. The keeper was named Bill. Bill was glad to have some company as he had been on duty for quite a long time. He was pulling a double to cover someone else's duty shift. He shared that he would be off for a while after a day or so more. That depended on when his replacement would arrive. Bill guided them to the lounge area and asked them to make themselves comfortable. They stood there for a couple minutes surveying the room. There were overstuffed chairs, end tables, and a wall of electronics, including stereo, reel-to-reel, and large television. The speakers were enormous.

Once they decided to pick a seat and get comfortable, Bill asked them if they were hungry. They told him that they were famished. The keeper vanished into another room; he reappeared a few minutes later with a large platter with steak, lobster tails, baked potatoes, garlic bread, and salads. The condiments were on a smaller tray. He then asked them what they would have to drink. John observed that they had their situation change from desperate to being waited on hand and foot. It was almost unbelievable. Red was thinking the same thing and commented that it only happens in the movies. After the boys had finished their banquet, the plates and all other items were placed on the serving tray and taken away. They were then served dessert and sweet tea. After removing the dessert tray, Bill came back into the room and got comfortable to converse with the boys.

Bill asked them how they got themselves in such a situation. John informed Bill of all the preparations he made in support of this weekend. He explained that it started out as a shakedown cruise for a couple hours on Friday afternoon. John then expressed that all was not lost as they had two days remaining to enjoy before going back to work on the July 5. The keeper looked confused. He stated that today is the Fourth of July. John and Red stated disbelief in unison. They could not believe a day was lost. What had happened to Sunday? Then Bill asked them to tell the complete story to him.

After the story was conveyed, Bill gave them a knowing nod. Bill shared the complete story of the Bermuda Triangle. He strongly suggested that it is real and seems to have strange effects from time to time. Many things cannot be explained. He surmised that they were caught up in the strange effects that caused all your batteries to go dead for no apparent reason. He suggested that they take a nap, and he would see if he could do something with their batteries. He told them he would wake them in the morning. Red and John fell asleep minutes later. Meanwhile, Bill went out to the boat and placed the main two batteries on trickle charge.

The boys woke up at the same time. It was 6:50 a.m., just early enough to see the sun coming up over the horizon. Bill appeared and handed them a cup of coffee each. He told the boys that he had placed the batteries on trickle charge for forty-five minutes, and they were now at full charge. The flashlights were working. "I did not charge the flashlight batteries." He told them that he tried to start the motor, and it cranked and started like a new motor. John and Red said nothing but just looked at each other. John just scratched his head as he would when confused.

After finishing his coffee, John jumped into the boat and picked up a flashlight. He turned it on, and the light was very bright. All three guys looked at each other and shook their heads in disbelief. John and Red each shook Bill's hand and thanked him for all his help with the boat and the fine food. Bill conveyed to the boys that he received a call from the coast guard on the ship-to-shore radio. "Your families are looking for you, boys. The coast guard was told that you are here, and they should have contacted your parents by now."

The boys got into the boat and started the motor. When they were ready to leave the dock, Bill threw the last line into the boat. They all waved as the boat was heading for the Black Creek boat ramp. Bill had placed a chart into the captain's cubbyhole. Red knew how to get to the boat ramp from there, so John had him operate the boat. The boys were calmed a bit and decided to stop on the way and do some fishing for a short while. Red set the throttle to trolling speed, and John put a pole in for himself and Red.

Both poles caught fish at the same time. Red put the motor on idle and reeled in his fish. They caught several fish that way in a short time. They decided to head for the Black Creek boat ramp. They were almost up to speed when the marine patrol detained them. They questioned them and checked their identification. They contacted Bill, and their story was verified. The marine patrol checked out the boat for safety and then told them all was fine and they could go on their way. They finally arrived back at the boat ramp after their strange adventure. They still could not figure how they lost one full day. John jumped out of the boat and pulled the truck and trailer back onto the boat ramp to put the boat on the trailer. They stopped on the way home and bought a cooler and ice for the fish.

When they arrived at John's parents' house, several friends and family greeted them. They were quizzed about what all happened and where they had been for three days. They said very little but said they were so glad to have people who were concerned about them. They conveyed to all that they had fresh fish to clean. After the fish were cleaned, Red went home.

John's parents asked him what happened. When he shared the adventure and that one lost day, his parent exchanged looks to each other and said something like, *All righty then.*

John realized that they probably thought that he was not telling the truth or the whole story. If he told them about the UFOs he and Red followed around the other night, they would probably commit him. John's mom cooked the fish and made hush puppies and french fries. The salads were better than the one at the lighthouse. John called Red to come eat some fish. Red came and had a fine meal. He enjoyed the food and the company of the ladies and other people who came to see that he and John were all right. Being lost for several days seems to make some people friendlier toward you. John's girlfriend kept so close to him as if he might get lost in the house or yard.

Red left for home early that evening. John went to bed early also as he was very tired from the adventure. The next evening, John arrived home from work and called Red. He asked him to come over and decide on something to do. Red did not want to leave his house. Red said John slept several hours while they were stranded in the boat, but he did not sleep a wink. Red would not discuss what happened or what he saw during that time. Red became paranoid and nervous. He withdrew from everyone. Red would talk strangely on the phone after that day.

At some point, his parents decided to admit him for a mental evaluation. John started traveling all over the country for work a short time after this adventure. John wondered why he did not seem to be affected by the adventure as Red was. John's strength and fortitude seemed to have been strengthened as a result. John has since read and heard a lot about the Devil's/ Bermuda Triangle since the adventure with the boat. He thought he might know most of what happened on the boat but still cannot figure out what actually happened to the one lost day.

6
THE LONG WAY HOME

John was working at a nuclear power generating plant construction site in the fall of 1980. He had recently been divorced after a marriage that lasted five years. He had been so saddened by his lovely wife not being committed or trustworthy. He was trying to move on with his life.

He was an inspector at the project and was currently assigned to monitor the blasting efforts of the contractor. He was to set up his monitoring equipment on the closest critical structure. The location this time was a tank base of concrete, which was a couple of feet larger in diameter than the tank installed on top of the slab. John had monitored placement and logged all the sticks of dynamite the contractor had placed into each predrilled hole. They were trying to remove the rock from the area to enable routing of the main piping to get them to the cooling towers for cooling. The shot preparations were completed, and the heavy mats were placed carefully over the blast area. The mats were very big and heavy. Several mats were placed as John set up his monitoring equipment. After preparing all day for the blast area to be shot, it was now time. An all-clear was conveyed, and the blasting horns were sounded for the required amount of time.

The shot area included a mud seam between the rock deposits, which was not noticed by John as he surveyed the area during his inspection and monitoring. The mud seams are sometimes not detectable until after the blast.

The shot was ignited, and all the millisecond-timed blasting caps were fired as planned. All the blast area was shot. John was at the side of the tank and thought he was safe from the blast. The mud and small rocks went through the holes in the steel mats and found John. John protected the machine and blast velocity tape. The mud fell all over his back and hard hat. The tank was also spotted with the mud. The contractor realized that John was safe and not injured. The superintendent laughed out loud at the mud-spotted inspector John.

John picked up his equipment and put it away in the company truck. He removed all the big chunks of mud from his hard hat and coveralls. He removed the coveralls and threw them into the bed of the truck and got inside to go to the site lab. He put the equipment away in the lab for the weekend as it was Friday and time to go home until Monday morning.

John washed and got ready to go home. He walked to his Triumph motorcycle, parked in the administrative parking lot. John had started his 750-cc motor and commenced to put on his helmet and tighten the chin strap. His motorcycle was kept clean and polished. He loved to ride it and was proud of how nice and clean it was kept. His motor had warmed, and John was about to head for home. A blue Corvette pulled up behind John and stopped. It belonged to his friend Sharky. He worked on the project too as a crane operator. He was finished with work as well and was on his way off site but saw John and stopped to talk to him.

Sharky informed John that there would be a live band playing at the Roadhouse Truck Stop later. The band was to start playing by eight o'clock that evening. The time was already almost six o'clock. They both decided to meet there at seven o'clock and have dinner then stay to meet some girls and dance with them to the music of the band.

The Roadhouse Truck Stop was located over a mile from the power plant site to the south. The state route went through Indiana from Jeffersonville to the north through Madison. John was staying in Jeffersonville at that time. John planned to stay a short time after dinner and then go home. He had heard a few bands play there before and was not impressed with the level of talent of the bands that usually played on the weekends.

John had decided to ride his motorcycle around the countryside for a while and then go to the roadhouse. He was truly enjoying his ride as the weather was excellent, and he had no traffic on the road but him. The early fall evening was progressing into the start of a beautiful sunset. John realized the time was getting late. He was to meet his friend around seven o'clock, and it was a little after the hour. He was not very far from the roadhouse and turned to take a back-road shortcut to get there before he would be much later.

John arrived at the roadhouse around seven thirty and saw that Sharky was already there. He saw his blue Corvette and parked his motorcycle close by. John put his kickstand down as he turned off his ignition and fuel petcock to his gas tank. He got off his motorcycle and started loosening his chin strap to remove his helmet. He opened the door and immediately spotted Sharky at an interior table sitting with two pretty girls.

Sharky stood up and waved John to his table. John proceeded to the table to join his friend and the two very pretty ladies. Sharky introduced everyone, and the guys each sat down in a chair at the table. John was a bit hungry and asked for a menu.

They all ordered and talked about many things while waiting for the food to arrive. They all got to know one another a bit and had a great dinner. The cook was above average, and the food was worth traveling a distance to enjoy. Dinner was drawing to a close. John ordered drinks all around the table. John's first beer went down quickly, and he ordered another. John's second beer was not half empty when the band started to play music.

The band and dance floor were both in another part of the building. They all decided to dance and left the table. They all continued to dance until the band stopped to take a break. The table was again regained, and they ordered another round of drinks. The band took a thirty-minute break, allowing all four people at the table to have a couple of drinks. The dancing, talking, and drinking continued through the evening.

The girls decided to stop drinking around ten-thirty as they had to drive home, not knowing how much longer they would stay before leaving for home. The girls stayed until the band played their last song for the night. John and Sharky danced every dance with the ladies. The dancing was over, and the girls were to go home. John and Sharky walked them to their car. After a good-night kiss, the girls said good-bye. John was given a phone number of one of the girls. The boys had not stopped drinking as the girls had earlier that night. John carried his helmet outside with him to see the girls off toward their home.

John got onto his motorcycle and watched the girls' car disappear into the night. Sharky turned to John after watching the girls leave. He asked John to come in and have something to eat before going home. A few cups of coffee were also mentioned. John shook his head negatively and kick-started his motor. Sharky said that was the wrong answer and tried to convince

John to come in and have a cup of coffee as a minimum. John said, "Another time, but not now." And he put his kickstand in the up position.

John was determined to leave. Sharky was worried about the amount of alcohol that had been consumed by John through the night. Sharky asked John once again to come back inside the all-night diner and have something. John said no and started to raise his foot to put the motorcycle in gear. Sharky realized there was no other way to help him, so he punched John. John did a back roll off the seat to end up on the parking lot in the sitting position.

John started laughing loudly. He was surprised that Sharky had hit him. John asked Sharky why he hit him. Sharky conveyed that John was very hardheaded, and he had to get his attention. Sharky had caught the motorcycle from falling over and put the kickstand back down. He also turned off the ignition and placed the keys in his pocket. He told John he could get the keys back after he ate something and was all right to navigate to his house. Sharky bent down to take John's hand and help him to his feet. They went in the door to the same table and had a meal and several cups of coffee.

After they finished their late meal and several cups of coffee, they looked at the clock on the wall. The clock displayed four o'clock in the morning. John was feeling normal and a bit tired. He was more than ready to go home. John stood up and informed Sharky that he was intending to head home. Sharky stood up and extended his hand to shake John's hand. He apologized to John for hitting him. John told him that he knew Sharky meant well, and it was no big deal. John agreed that he was being hardheaded. They walked to the parking lot together, and John received his keys from Sharky. John started his motorcycle and reached back to get his leather jacket. The air was cool. As he zipped his leather jacket, he heard the Corvette start. It sounded so strong.

John watched the Corvette turn into the state road to the north as he finished fastening his chin strap to his helmet. He put the shifter into first gear and eased the clutch out, starting down the road to the south toward his present home. John ensured the kickstand was all the way in the up position and went smoothly through the gears. John had over fifteen miles to ride to get home. He was glad that he had zipped his jacket up since the night air was cool. He was enjoying the ride. The new moon seemed to cause the night to be darker than usual. A fog was setting in the low areas of the roadway.

John was traveling south at around seventy miles per hour with no traffic on the road but him. He noticed a diamond-shaped yellow sign ahead, denoting a sharp curve to the right. A second later, John noticed car lights approaching him very fast. The lights were in front of him and in his lane. In a second, he realized the car was in his lane and was about to hit him. The car had cut the inside of the curve, and there he was.

John made a split-second decision and went off to the shoulder of the road, in time to be missed by the car by inches. His eyes caught a glimpse of the car to notice it was red. As soon as the car had passed by, the sign was not very far ahead. He was approaching it quickly and made a decision to get his motorcycle back onto the roadway. There was several inches difference between the low-shoulder elevation and the roadway surface. When he leaned to get the motorcycle back onto the roadway surface, the tires climbed the side of the pavement onto the roadway. The yellow curve sign was missed and was passed with little time or distance to spare. The front tire was immediately into an area of fine rocks as small as coarse sand.

The clean and shiny Triumph motorcycle was about to go down. John had raced motorcycles and had crashed before. He threw his leg up on the seat to ride it down to the pavement. The front wheel was turned a little to one side. The front wheel went through the fines to suddenly find clean solid pavement. The motorcycle slowed down abruptly, and John's momentum carried him on and over the handlebars onto the pavement of the state road. His knee hit the handlebars as he went over and straightened the course of the motorcycle. John was now sliding down the pavement with the asphalt surface rubbing the skin from his hands, arms, cheeks, legs and disintegrating his leather jacket.

John was finally slowing down and hurting all over. He was so glad no other traffic was on the road when the front tire of his motorcycle found him, running up his back and over his right shoulder. The back tire followed and ran up his back but, taking a slightly different course, ran over his head. The back tire had most of the weight of the motorcycle on it, which crushed and split the Bell brand helmet he was wearing. John was going to probably walk away from the situation until he suffered a severe concussion, or worse. John could not move at all. Then he blacked out.

John was in the middle of the road with his motorcycle crashed into the trees at the eastside of the road. A man was driving to Madison at around five o'clock. He lived in Jeffersonville but worked in Madison. He came upon John sprawled on the roadway and stopped a few inches from him. His car stopped sideways in the road. He had been issued a cellular phone by his company just days before. He called for the police and an ambulance. He pulled John from the middle of the road to the side and checked his pulse. He informed the lady on the phone that John's pulse was very weak.

About twenty minutes after he called, the ambulance arrived. The police arrived a few minutes later. The family man from Jeffersonville left for work shortly after the ambulance arrived. The emergency technician thanked him for moving John to the side of the road and checking his pulse. The emergency technicians both worked together to get John into the ambulance on the bed. They realized that John was in really serious shape.

While all of this was happening with John, he knew nothing about it. John was experiencing a bright light. He was feeling so deeply at peace. He had a strong feeling of being asked a question, if he wanted to go or stay. Before he answered the question, it dawned on him that his leaving this world would sadden many people, especially his family. John asked to stay alive and to please allow his injuries to heal. The response he felt was that it was granted, that he wanted to stay as he had not finished much of what he was here to do. He had the feeling that he was being told that he had things he was put on earth to do that were not yet accomplished.

During this time, the emergency technicians were on their way to the hospital with John. They were contacting the hospital by two-way radio and trying to keep John alive. The doctor at the hospital was directing Donna to tell Sharon to use the defibrillator on John to get his heart working correctly. This conversation happened several times as his heart kept stopping. They called him in as DOA three different times. Then his heart would start beating again each time.

While they were trying to keep John alive, he was floating above them taking it all in. He was hearing and seeing it all, or most, of what was happening. John heard the doctor giving Donna directives that she conveyed for Sharon to perform. John felt so much at peace with it all as if it was happening to someone else. At some point John no longer hovered over them as they tried vigorously in a dedicated manner to keep him alive.

One week after arriving at a Jeffersonville hospital, John woke up in a private room. He had no memory. He knew nobody or who he was, where he was, or why he was there. His memory eluded him. For four to five weeks, he knew nothing as he had no recall of his memory or people he should know. People who came to visit were all strangers to him. Two of his sisters came to visit, and he did not recognize them.

One day about two weeks after arriving in the hospital, he received a visit by the emergency technicians who had helped keep him alive from the side of the road in the country to the hospital in Jeffersonville. Donna first arrived to visit John. When she entered John's room, he called her by name. Donna passed out into a nearby chair. The nurse who accompanied her caught her, ensuring she did not hit the floor. The nurse quickly acquired some smelling salts and revived Donna.

Donna looked at John inquisitively and asked him how he knew her name. At that moment, Sharon, the other emergency technician, came through the door and entered his room. He said hello to Sharon, calling her by name, and she had to find a seat next to Donna. Sharon required some smelling salts to overcome her dizziness from becoming overwhelmed. Sharon asked John how he knew her name, and Donna told her that he knew her name as well. John told them of the bright light and the question presented to him. He informed them of his answers and then conveyed his hovering above them as they worked on him.

Their eyes got very large and their mouths wide open as they took it all in, trying to make sense of it all. John conveyed how he watched them performing their duties. He explained that he watched Donna on the two-way radio receiving instructions and conveying the doctor's instructions to Sharon. He conveyed the call-in to the doctor when there were no positive results. He conveyed the relief they exhibited when he started breathing again on his own.

Sharon said that he had not regained consciousness during the trip, and it all doesn't make sense. John scratched his head then shared that it was a first for him and laughed. The doctor entered the room in time to hear John's explanation to the girls. The doctor scratched his head and stated that the story was a first for him, but he had heard other stories that he did not understand that had supposedly occurred in the past.

The doctor said that he could not understand how John could recall all the facts he just conveyed but could not remember his own name or any of his friends or relatives who had visited him. The doctor conveyed that John had known some of his visitors all his life. Yet John remembered the two emergency technicians by name and described every action they performed in detail. They were all baffled and left together a few minutes after the discussion was over as the visit terminated.

John's ear was sewn back in place after the visit. He was not expected to live prior to the visit. The doctor could not explain John's remembering only certain things but realized that John was going to continue to live for a time. John had been in a coma for over a week and suddenly woke up. The doctor told John that he would sew the ear back straight if he stayed still. John did not move a muscle, although he felt some of the stitches as they were performed.

Five weeks had passed since the night of the accident, and John started recalling things. Sharky came to visit him, and John remembered him. Others came to visit John since he was beginning to remember things and people. By the end of the fifth week, John was released. Sharky took John home from the hospital. John informed Sharky that the car had ran him off the road, and it had nothing to do with anything that occurred earlier that night. Sharky informed John that his Triumph was totaled and not worth repairing. John seemed not to mind. John explained the total experience to Sharky on the ride to John's house.

Sharky just looked at John and said nothing. Sharky did not know what to think about it all. John informed Sharky that the doctor informed him that he could have no form of alcohol for a minimum of six months or longer. The trauma John's head suffered would cause him to black out and could cause worse issues. Sharky was all for waiting six months minimum for his friend to drink again.

John told only a few people about his experiences that late night and early morning on the state route in Indiana on his way home in Jeffersonville. His life seemed to have more substance and direction. He got off track a few times after that but managed to pull himself back on the right path in a short time. John was so glad that the emergency technicians had visited him that day to verify what he thought were real experiences. He was then assured that it had all happened.

These experiences caused John to reevaluate many things and where he was headed in his life. The issues with his ex-wife that had torn him no longer seemed to bother him as it had until then. His child whom his wife kept away from him would someday remember his loving ways toward her and seek to find her dad. He began seeking God as it became more his desire and trying to live as God would approve. John realized that there was so much we do not know or understand, and he wanted to try to learn and realize all about God to the degree that he would be able to understand His ways. John believed that he had been given a second chance.

7
HOUSE FOR SALE

John was living in Jeffersonville while working a nuclear power plant construction project as a construction engineering inspector. He had suffered a serious motorcycle accident several months before. He was not to drink any alcohol for six months minimum due to the massive concussion he had suffered in the accident.

John had decided to continue working on the project although he had received offers from several other companies that required additional qualified personnel on projects elsewhere. Sharky was a very good friend of John's. He tried to convince John to go to another project with him as the pay rate was much higher. Illinois was not a state that John thought he wanted to live or work on a project. John had decided to stay where he was for a while longer.

John and Sharky took a trip to Ohio to buy a car from John's sister. She had a car to sell, and John had a hard time getting around, since his motorcycle was wrecked and found to be a total loss. They had a great fun weekend in Ohio and followed each other back to Indiana. Sharky left a week later to go to his new job in Illinois.

John worked with several people within his company on the project. One guy named Kit was separated from his wife and needed a roommate to help with the bills. It seemed that since his wife left to move back with her mother in New England, Kit needed more funds to support his nightlife and have money to send to his wife. He also had to pay the rent on the house and other bills. John was asked by Kit to move in with him and split the rent and utilities. Kit lived five miles from the site. John was driving over twenty miles to work. The closer place to live was a good thing and cheaper than his monthly expenses at that time.

John thought about Kit's offer for a couple days and then told Kit he would move in. They went to Kit's after work, and John reviewed the house and his room he would be renting. They came to an agreement, and John planned to move in the following weekend.

The weekend was also a pay week as John's company paid every two weeks. All was seemingly looking up for John. John informed his landlord of his moving out on the coming weekend. Early that Saturday morning, John packed his car and dropped off the keys to the rental. He arrived at Kits before nine in the morning and woke Kit while trying to carry his clothes in to the room that was to be his. The house was a two-bedroom house and was very nice. John finished moving in and took a shower. Kit took a shower while John was organizing his room.

Kit and John decided to go to town to have lunch in Madison. Kit had a Pontiac Grand Prix, and John liked that brand of car. Kit offered to use his car to go to lunch. John and Kit went to Madison to have lunch in the Grand Prix. The restaurant was nice and was part of a complex that includes a motel and a large lounge that had live bands on the weekends. Kit knew the owner and introduced John to the owner. She was a pretty lady and very nice person. Her name was Maye. John decided that he would eat at her restaurant often, since the food was fine, and it was not far from where he now lived.

John and Kit drove their own vehicles to work as they would get off at different times from their assignments. Kit tried to get off early to go home, get ready, and go out to chase girls most nights. Kit's nightlife was the cause for his wife leaving. The girlfriends multiplied in number after his wife left to live with her parents.

The next Friday evening was a rare occasion with Kit and John getting home at the same time. Kit asked John if he wanted to double date with him and his lady. John called a lady he had met at the restaurant in Madison a couple days before. The lady accepted the date, and the guys got ready. Kit decided to take his car. They picked up the ladies and then announced that they were going to go dancing after they went to a house that was for sale at that time. All agreed to the plan. Then Kit conveyed the fact that people say that the house is haunted and has been for sale for a long time. The girls got suddenly quiet. John told the girls that they were protected and can leave when they decide. The girls were happy with that arrangement. They all rode toward the old plantation house outside of town. The time was a couple hours before dark. They decided that they had plenty of time before dark to walk through and leave the house in the daylight.

It was a few minutes outside of Madison to the old plantation house. They waited for Kit to park the car. They were sizing up the situation with this big old house before they wanted to exit the car. Kit brought Mary, and John brought Jane. Both girls were dressed in designer jeans with very pretty blouses that almost matched. The guys had on dungarees and golf shirts. They all were wearing sports shoes, which seemed to be better for dancing and touring an old vacant house. John was the first one from the car, prompting Jane to join him. He tried to convince her that it was just a big old house. She decided that she was being a bit silly and joined John. Kit got out of the car and convinced Mary to join him. The four of them walked around the outside of the old mansion. It was a very majestic house in years gone by. John was entertaining thoughts of buying the house and trying to fix it up. That was his thoughts prior to taking the tour.

Around the back of the house were more structures built on, continuing for many attached buildings. The kitchen, maid's quarters, and wood and metal shop facilities were some of the added-on and attached structures. Some of the tools were still there. The tools were old hand tools with no power tools to be found. There were big cast-iron pots that could be hung over the hearth or placed on a large wooden stove. The old kitchen utensils, pots, and kettles were interesting. All of them showed wear from use. They spent over half an hour reviewing the built-on buildings attached to the house. There was a big barn in the back of the house a distance away. The tall weeds and brush was a deterrent that kept them all four from venturing there for a look. They decided the ticks and snakes were probably plentiful around that old barn.

They all glanced toward the old mansion, and Kit led the way toward the back of the house. John made eerie noises behind Jane, and she jumped and turned around with her eyes as big as saucers. John burst into laughter. Jane saw little humor and smacked John on to arm. Jane suggested that he quit the noises if they were to go inside the old house. John promised not to make anymore scary noises.

The door was unlocked. When Kit twisted the knob, the door opened with a loud squeak and dragged across the floor as he pushed the door open. The house was settling along the back door as a minimum. The room was huge and seemed as big as a normal house's combined total space. The doorways were arched and had beautiful wood trim that continued around the room on the walls for two feet up from the floor. The wall covering looked to be of a silk material. The ceiling had woodwork trim around the room at the ceiling that went down the walls for close to a foot-and-a-half and onto the ceiling for a distance of eight inches.

The group went through the massive room to the double archway at one end of the room. They followed single file through the double archway and were again amazed at the large staircase that went up to the second floor. The front room was very large as well. They walked through the downstairs from one end to the other. The windows were extra large and had beautiful wooden sills and carved wood along the vertical sides of each window and along the top. The windowsills were carved and had a carved border below each window. The center windows had stained glass. The sun shining through the glass made extremely interesting patterns and beautiful colors onto the walls and ceilings. The floors in the house on the first floor were all marble, and the ceilings were sculpted plaster. They were really impressed with the old house.

John said that he had seen all the downstairs rooms and wanted to check out the second floor. John led the way. Jane was close behind him with Mary behind her, and Kit at the end of the line, trailing up the ornate staircase. They went to the far end of the second floor where they found the door closed. The door had stained glass in it, and it was making beautiful patterns on the hallway wall and ceiling. The room was very large, and the sculpted plaster ceiling was falling with some already fallen onto the hardwood parquet floor and was gone from half of the ceiling in the room. The roof was leaking. John looked into the closets and found more of the same damage from the leaking roof.

They decided to stay together and exited the room into the hall. They went through all the upstairs rooms and the closets. They found that the far end room they went into first was the only one with water damage. Then they came to the room at the top of the stairs. Its windows faced the front yard and overlooked the side driveway somewhat. They could see Kit's car in the side drive if they looked out the window at an angle. They all had a problem getting the door to the room open. There was no apparent reason for the door to be so hard to open. They were finally in the room after the boys pushed hard against the door, and it finally opened.

The room was the smallest of them all. There were fireplaces in each room. The fireplace in this room was sealed with brick. There was a closet door, and another door, several feet from the closet door that seemed to possibly be an access door to the attic. Kit opened the closet door, and nothing at all was there. It was the smallest closet they had seen in the house. Kit was in the way of the other door. John asked him to open the door or move to the side so he could open it to see where it went. Kit moved to the side, and John opened the door. It took some effort as it did not open easily. That door did not drag but was reluctant to open for some reason.

The door opened to reveal a stairwell going up, winding to the right to be continuing out of sight, seeming to continue above the ceiling of the room. The stairs were narrow, and no light could illuminate the staircase from outside. The stairs went straight for many steps and then started the turn to the right. John and Jane started up the stairs. They noticed a short panel door on the left in the staircase above the second-floor ceiling. John thought it was an access door for a storage space. When John tried to open the small door, a sound of a low growling started being heard by all in the staircase. It seemed to John to be coming from wind around the chimney that was routed through the space from the fireplace below into the room.

The door was opened wide after Kit had gone to the car to get a flashlight and returned. Kit gave the flashlight to John. The light was shined into the space behind the small door. The growling sound was suddenly louder than it had been. John asked Mary to check to see if the wind was blowing outside. She went to the window and saw the tree leaves were dead still. She did not know if she should tell them that there was no wind at all. John shined the flashlight into the space and saw it would be tight to get access into the little room. The light hit a long rectangular black item in the space to the right side of the small but seemingly long room. It seemed to have brass in places on the side he could see. Jane said that the object looked a lot like a casket.

The noise was getting louder, and the bedroom door slammed shut. John looked at Kit and the girls and then slammed the small access door shut. Mary decided to tell John that there was not any wind outside, as they were all trying to climb down the staircase. They were finally down the narrow dimly lit staircase and back in the room and looking at each other. John slammed the door shut. John went to the door of the small room and grabbed the doorknob on the door to exit the room and pulled very hard. His hand slipped off. He placed both hands on the door and had to brace his leg against the wall beside the door for leverage. The door came open. The noise from the small room at the end of the stairs could be heard loudly by all and gaining volume.

John turned the door loose and turned to talk to Kit. The door slammed closed again. It took Kit and John both to get the door back open. The girls were more than ready to leave the room and the house. The boys held the door as the girls exited the room. Then they went out of the room one at a time. The girls quickly began descending the main staircase to the first floor once they exited the small room with the moaning sounds. Kit was right behind them. John was last and started to comment to the others as he approached the main staircase.

As John left the room, the door slammed shut very hard behind him. He was going to let them know that the noise stopped when they were all out of the room, and the door was closed to the room again but not by him.

Before he could say anything, he felt a very strong push from behind him as he stepped onto the second step down the staircase. The others were a few steps from the bottom floor landing when they turned to see John act as if he was pushed very hard from the back, falling down the stairs. It was no act as he tumbled down the stairs. The girls and Kit jumped to the side to avoid being hit by a tumbling body. John stopped at the bottom of the staircase on his shoulder. His body was bruised, and he had a few knots on his head as well. They were lucky to get out of his way as he tumbled down the staircase.

They helped John up to his feet and asked him if he was all right and if anything was broken. John was very athletic and lucky this day. They stood there looking over John to ensure he was all right, and then the growling sound started again, louder than before. They all looked at each other and said that they were getting out of the house. The front door would not open. Kit was desperately trying to open the front door with the girls helping. John limped a little as he continued to the end door closest to where the car was parked outside in the side driveway.

John tried the door, and it opened with one hand and little effort. He called to the others, and they all walked very briskly to the door where John was standing, holding the door open for them all to exit the growling house. Once they were all back in the car and the car had started, they were ready to talk very loudly about it all. As they sit in the car discussing how it might have been their imagination, John noticed a very pale figure in the upstairs bedroom window staring at them. The pale figure of a person lit a cigarette while all were checking him out, as John had brought the pale figure to their attention a moment before. They all then told Kit to drive away from the house fast. The figure in the upstairs bedroom was visible to them all as it watched them speed down the drive to leave the property. The figure was hard to see at the angle it was at to view in the car in the side driveway, but it could be seen clearly as the car went down the drive and to the county road.

The majestic old house and all the buildings were demolished a few months after their visit. That made John a bit sad when he heard about it. The house was beautiful at one time. John also knew that it was haunted, and he could not buy the property, and the house required much repair. John did not desire to go downstairs at a speed such as that ever again. They went to a lounge that had a live band and had drinks, danced and talked about the strange house for sale. John decided to have a soda.

Maybe it was imaginations gone wild or a haunted house. Now we will never know. John and Kit did not really want to ever go back to the property even though the house was torn down.

8
NIGHT SKY OVER DALLAS

In the fall of 1985, John went to Dallas, Texas, to visit his dad and other relatives of his dad's side of the family. John visited for several days as he had time between projects and had not seen his dad for quite some time. John traveled to many states for work. Every project seemed to require another move to a place he had not lived before.

This day John and his dad were to travel around the Dallas area to visit relatives. They were in the car driving to the first aunt's house shortly after breakfast. They were in his dad's 1976 Pontiac Grand Prix. It was a comfortable ride. John thought his next car should be a car like his dads.

It seemed that all of John's relatives were excessively busy, and some of them were not home when John and his dad arrived. Notes were left on their door by John and then on to the next destination. John's dad had been very busy working long hours since moving to Dallas after his divorce from John's mother several years before. They had been married for twenty-two years, and their divorce devastated John as well for a while. Life has a way of helping people get over or through things that negatively impact them. It is called making a living and trying to better life's situations. Some people get lost or absorbed into the effort of life and support issues. John submerged himself in his work for several years. He realized the people and things he missed and neglected for that lost time. That was one reason for this trip. John understood very well why his dad kept himself so busy.

They returned back to the apartment complex where John's dad and other relatives lived in North Dallas. They had planned to visit relatives close by his dad's home last this day. It was close to dark when they visited the last family of relatives. They lived in an apartment complex at the edge of the complex grounds. The perimeter of the property overlooked a portion of the downtown in the city of Dallas. John and his dad visited his aunt and uncle for over an hour in their apartment at the perimeter of the grounds. Once they said their good-byes and exited the apartment, the view of Dallas from the overlook attracted John's interest. John and his dad walked over to the edge of the property overlooking Dallas and viewed the lights and activity for a while. It had turned to night while they were visiting inside their relatives' home. The weather was fine with a very faint breeze and a full moon. The sky was clear, and the stars could be seen way above the lights of the city below.

John and his dad were discussing the weather and vastness of the city below. John saw what seemed to be a cloud bank to the east from the corner of his left eye. He turned his head to view the approaching clouds. He was amazed to see a very large craft approaching from the east, seeming to be quietly floating directly over downtown Dallas, not making a sound. John told his dad to look up at the sky. He pointed at the craft. His dad said that it was probably a craft of some kind from the army base to the west of Dallas.

John was in awe as he watched the craft floating quietly across the Dallas night sky. His dad was a World War II veteran who still lived by the motto "loose lips sink ships" patriotic attitude. John conveyed to his dad that he knew of the science of canceling noise by producing negative sound waves of the same frequency. He never had occasion to witness the theory in practice before now. John decided that had to be why no sound could be heard.

As the very large strange craft continued to float across the night sky, John stated that it had grid lines and gigantic pipes visible, seeming to turn in to the interior of the craft. There were no markings on the craft that was larger than a super oil tanker. It was rectangular in shape and was wider than a couple football fields and more than ten times that dimension in length as a minimum. It seemed to be twenty stories or more from the bottom to the top of the craft on the side passing by him. It was hard to decide accurate dimensions when you are looking at a strange craft floating by at approximately five thousand feet in the air, not making a sound. It had no visible propulsion system or landing gears. The craft had no markings on the areas that he could see. It seemed that John and his dad were the only people in all of Dallas, and maybe all of Texas, who saw the craft.

It took over one-half hour for the strange craft to pass from the corner of John's eye to get too small to clearly note as it continued to the west. John and his dad watched until the craft appeared very small in the western sky, and the view became obstructed by tree limbs. John and his dad decided to go to the apartment and take his dad's dog out for a walk. John and his dad briefly discussed the craft, and then his dad changed the subject. John was not sure that his dad had not seen the craft before. His dad started a discussion about what John's plans were and when he was planning to leave the next day, for his trip to his new project. John knew the conversation about the strange craft had ended.

John woke up earlier than his dad and took a shower. He packed and was close to being ready to leave before his dad was up and planning breakfast. John had already made coffee and drank almost half of the pot. They went out together to walk the dog, and then John packed his 63 Chevy. He said good-bye to his dad and his dad's dog and left for his new project.

John never saw the strange craft again. He often thought about the experience of the sighting and recalled how his dad was not shocked or overly excited about seeing the craft. John always would somewhat believe that his dad had seen the craft before. It seemed commonplace to his dad that night. John would visit his dad every now and then, and the subject of the strange craft would come up. His dad would converse about it for a short while and then change the subject.

There was nothing John or his dad could do about the craft. They had no physical evidence. The government has not presented that type of craft to the public at air shows. If it was a government craft, they would probably deny its existence, since it had no visible way to maintain altitude or propel the craft in any direction. The craft could be used to transport a town or small city's population with ease to somewhere. It was so quiet that nobody would know the craft was traveling through their area, unless they looked up to see the strange craft silently float across the sky.

John still to this day wonders what kind of propulsion system the craft had to keep it moving and enables it to maintain an altitude. The newspaper and news broadcasts the next day had no mention of the craft being sighted by anyone. It is almost as if it was John's imagination or a vivid dream. But John knows better.

www.ingramcontent.com/pod-product-compliance
Ingram Content Group UK Ltd.
Pitfield, Milton Keynes, MK11 3LW, UK
UKHW022216230426
12048UKWH00016BA/890